OBSERVATIONS
FROM A
THIRD-STORY
WINDOW

AND OTHER STORIES

ZACHARY A. CALAIS

Printed in the United States of America

ISBN-13   978-0-6159773-7-9
ISBN-10   0-615977-375

REVISED EDITION

TO NATHAN

You taught me how to make an instant last forever,
and how to collapse eternity into a single moment in time

CONTENTS

MY LIFE AS A FAIRY TALE

PREFACE

This is a work of fiction. While I do choose to draw *inspiration* not only from the "characters" around me, as well as the events which have occurred throughout my everyday life, everything found here did spring forth from my imagination.

In fact, the stories collected here were never intended for publication, much less in a single volume. Most were created while I was stranded, hopelessly bored, in airports, seminars, conference rooms, family gatherings, *et cetera, et cetera, et cetera.*

While it may have not been my intention to publish these stories at all, while working on another manuscript, I found myself hitting dead end after dead end. My home office had plummeted into a state of disorganization that often left me wondering if I should simply pour lighter fluid around the entire room, set it ablaze, and let the insurance company sort it out.

My husband, however, had a more practical approach. Having always been my biggest cheerleader, he has a unique way of motivating me. He did not innocently inquire as to whether or not I would collect the stories together and publish them. He skipped past surreptitiously submitting them to a publisher without my knowledge. Instead he, as usual, chose a different path.

He calmly gathered them into a stack, and threw them at my head.

When I opened my mouth to protest, he began admonishing me that, yes, I was wringing my hands over a book that had not come fully into form, much less be completed, yet here was one that was, in fact, not only complete, but the only productive thing it was doing was literally covering up the "disaster area you like to call a desk."

I learned two lessons that day:

First, my husband, once focused on a task, would hound a person until it was completed to his satisfaction, as opposed to theirs.

Second, attempted humor (such as, hypothetically, titling the book *My Husband Made Me Do It*) has multiple ramifications, not the least of which is being wished a good night's sleep on the couch.

Like everything else in this book, what you have read so far is (somewhat) fictional. While I have chosen to draw from my own life's experiences for inspiration, the characters have been aggrandized (or completely invented altogether), the events blown thoroughly out of proportion, and the imagery over-saturated to the point of utter sensory overload.

I am, and will always be, grateful to my many Muses for helping me bring this book into being. I am also grateful for my husband, for without him, life would merely be an existence, and I would be no better off than the protagonist of the titular story.

In addition, my husband has, throughout this entire process, taught me one other important lesson:

I will make damned sure I never leave any manuscript, whether finished or not, laying around the house again.

Zachary A. Calais
Atlanta, Georgia
Christmas Day, 2014

OBSERVATIONS
FROM A
THIRD-STORY
WINDOW

RICHARD CHARLES MCGLOMMER, IV, WAS A GOOD MAN. Fueled by routine, he showed up every day at nine a.m. sharp, he lunched exactly at noon, and left at five p.m. on the dot. He often worked weekends, maintaining his weekday routine, of course, and he never socialized with his co-workers outside of the office. His clothing, neither stylish nor garish, consisted of inexpensive fabrics in earth tones and cuts too large for his frame. His hair was once dark brown, and his baldness followed the pattern of every other male McGlommer who came before him: thinning first on top, then the bald spot expanding over the years, leaving him a only a dusted ring, the color of graying wood. When he retired, precisely at five o'clock on his sixtieth birthday, he picked up his briefcase, switched off the light in his office, and returned to the third-story walk-up apartment which had been his home his entire adult life. There, he set down his briefcase just inside the doorway to the kitchen, as if it were any other workday.

Retirement saw no change to his routine; he rose, showered and dressed, making himself presentable for the world precisely at nine o'clock. He soon discovered, however, that there was nothing for him to do. Having never married, there were neither children to criticize nor grandchildren to spoil. Having no social life, there were no friends with whom to catch up, or new friends to make. Instead, he withdrew from the world completely into the comforting embrace of his third-story apartment, with only the television and a never-used computer for company.

He still lunched precisely at noon, now at the small metal table in his kitchen instead of alone at the round, standard cafeteria one which had been placed furthest away from the window in the office lunchroom. The table in his kitchen, however, due to the law of function over form, required placement beneath the only window in the room. Richard could not remember ever having looked out this window before, and if he had been asked prior to his retirement, he would have assured his inquisitor that the window did not even exist. Through the window, Richard was offered a view of the single-block park across the street from his building which Richard could barely recall passing on his daily commute. Hardly used, the park was nothing more than a bench and a patchwork square of different grasses, surrounded by an overgrown hedge – a forgotten dollop of nature amongst the chrome, steel and concrete of the city.

It was late May. One day during his lunch (tuna salad on wheat), Richard looked out and was astonished to see two people in the park – quite possibly the first two people he had ever seen there. He looked down at his plate, then out the window again, and they were still there – two men. One was tall and slender, with spiky blond hair. His companion was slightly shorter, slightly darker, and slightly rounder – though his clothing seemed to be made for a much larger man. Richard watched in shock as they hesitantly touched, first their hands, then their bodies coming together in a full embrace. The Blond dipped his head slightly, catching the Dark One's mouth with his own in a kiss that, as it progressed, grew less and less chaste.

Richard quickly turned away, embarrassed at first. But intrigue overtook embarrassment, and soon he turned to look out the window once more.

They were gone.

As if they had vanished into thin air, all that was left were the bench and the patchwork grass and the overgrown hedge. Richard could not help but note that while the sudden disappearance of the men was jarring, even more unsettling was the fact that it was now well after one o'clock, almost two. His half-eaten sandwich, the bread stale and the tuna salad now room temperature, sat forgotten on his plate on the table against the wall in his kitchen in front of the window that looked over the small park.

The next day, Richard sat down with his lunch (bacon, lettuce and tomato on toasted wheat) precisely at noon, determined to finish it in the time allotted and be about his day long before the clock struck one. He had kept his focus on his plate for a five full minutes, when, in a rare moment of inattention, he glanced out the window and saw, once again, the Blond and the Dark One, seeming to glow in the midday light. There were no embraces today; quite the opposite, in fact. The two were circling each other as if they were sparring, but instead of exchanging blows, they seemed to be trading barbs. The Blond gesticulated wildly with his hands, while the Dark One preferred a more subdued approach. Richard watched with amazement as they drew close and drifted apart, almost rhythmically, seeming to dance around the square with practiced ease. Despite the ferocity of their motions, Richard could not detect a shred of animosity – here were two men who cared about each other enough to speak not only honestly, but be *brutally* honest while doing so.

Completely flustered, the Blond spun on a heel and began to stride stiffly out of the park, his tall, lanky frame almost mechanical in his motions. But when he reached the edge of the grass, he stopped suddenly. His exit had been watched woefully by his companion, but now there seemed to be an unasked question in the air. The Blond slowed his breathing, and turned to look at the Dark One. After the most pregnant of pauses, the Blond reached out a hand – a hand the Dark One did not hesitate to take. They walked out of the park and down the street together, still a small amount of distance between them, but their hands joined all the same.

The next day, as Richard returned to his window-side table, the couple returned to the small park across the street. Soon they settled into a daily routine, the two men would talk, argue, fight, or sometimes simply sit on the worn bench and hold each other. Every day their life played out before him, much like the television programs he used to fill the evenings of loneliness, but much more interesting. Despite the lack of sound, Richard was amazed how accurately he could interpret their growing relationship.

To look at the two, one would never surmise that they would be a couple. One older, one younger; one professional and educated, the other an obvious free spirit; one mostly conservative in dress, the other so outlandish Richard often wondered if the Blond shopped at every store ever opened in the history of man. One day he was restrained in jeans and a button-up shirt, and on the next he would be wearing shorts that accentuated his more… intimate features, shorts that were much shorter than any

Richard had ever seen. While he would never be caught dead in such attire, Richard could not deny that the Blond was stunningly beautiful.

Oddly, the Dark One never seemed to notice the Blond's beauty. Of course, one would have to be blind not to see it, but the Dark One seemed preoccupied with engaging the Blond's brain. Never had he seen two talk as these two – passionately, without abandon, and sometimes stepping on each other's sentences.

It was late summer, and a long drought had come to a close. Despite the constant downpour all morning, Richard once again took his place at the small table in the kitchen. Halfheartedly, he looked out the window, not expecting the men to brave the rain to maintain their daily ritual. To his amazement, there they were – just like any other day. He looked closer, and he swore he could see the rain ending at the edge of the square of green. It was hard to be certain through the curtain of water that poured from the sky, but both men appeared to be dry. Today's moment was tender, and Richard had to strain his eyes to make it out. The Blond was sitting with his back on the Dark One's chest, his head resting on his shoulder. For once, their conversation was not animated. At one point, the Blond turned and asked the Dark One a question, one which apparently greatly amused the Dark One. A single hand caressed the Blond's chin, and after a quick kiss directly on the lips – a simple kiss, short, direct, and lovingly delivered – the Dark One stared into the Blond's eyes and nodded his head, before pulling the younger man tightly to him.

At the time, Richard did not know what question had been asked, but he knew in that very moment that he had borne witness to something pivotal.

Matching rings appeared on their left hands early in the fall, when the leaves of the overgrown hedge began to turn from the verdant green to the dusty brown of winter, only to be reborn the following spring. Over the months, the Blond became a little less skinny, the Dark One a little less chunky. The Dark One's clothing began to change – as did that those of the Blond. Their appearances, once polar opposites, began to homogenize into a single theme, one that drew only the best parts of their individual styles. Together they created a new being—a wedded soul which proved that, on occasion, one plus one can equal much more than two.

For years, this daily routine was followed – neither the performers nor the audience abandoned their noontime commitment. Long gone was Richard's foreboding of being discovered. In fact, it did not appear that the couple never feared being seen at all. Passersby always managed to walk right by the park as if there were nothing there. Some days there were some very intimate moments shared in that park, moments it seemed to which Richard was the only, embarrassed voyeur.

How long had it been? Five years or ten? Four years or forty? Richard's only real connection to the world outside his window was through the lives of these two men – the Blond and the Dark One. When he had first retired, Richard had chosen not to leave his third-story apartment for fear of the world. Now, he could not leave for fear of his health. He had more visitors these days – nurses and caretakers mostly, but they were universally banished from the apartment during the noon hour.

That time was reserved for just the three of them.

Richard had grown so accustomed to his daily voyeurism that when the Blond and the Dark One did not show up one day – was it a Wednesday? – it hit him like an electric shock. A tightness began to grip his chest. Where were they? Was everything alright?

Assuring himself that they were simply meeting elsewhere and that they would return tomorrow, Richard went about the rest of the day, but his eyes kept flickering to the kitchen window more and more often. The next morning, Richard sat at the table at ten o'clock sharp, determined not to miss the men should their visit start early, or worse, be cut short.

Again, the Blond and the Dark One did not come.

Was the show over? How dare they do this to him? While the pair had not been his sole source of companionship, if one included the caretakers and the nurses, they had been the only ones who had led him to feel joy, happiness, and now fear in all the years since his retirement, since he had withdrawn from the world as a whole.

Every day for one month, then two, Richard sat at the table by the window in the kitchen of his third-story apartment, and every day for one month, then two, the two men did not appear. The nurses and caretakers began to use words like "difficult" and "stubborn." One caretaker went as far as to call Richard "crotchety," an appellation for which Richard did not care at all. The very next day, Richard had someone new to assist him.

Crotchety, indeed.

While he no longer prepared his own meals, he still, every day, took his lunch by the kitchen window. It was the middle of winter, the trees bare of their leaves, and while Richard could not feel the wind from inside his apartment, the park looked bitter and cold. Pedestrians outside were all bundled up in hats and coats and gloves, with scarves the only splash of color in the sea of browns and blacks and grays.

One midwinter's day, Richard was rewarded. He looked out the window, their window, and there on the bench sat the Dark One – he was sure of it, although his hair had grown shaggily unkempt, and the blond streak that he wore in the front had started to disappear into the dull, lifeless brown-black that made up the rest of his hair. Richard's eyes darted around the park, sure he would soon see the Blond – the beautiful Blond with the spiky hair.

But the Blond did not appear.

Richard looked closer at the Dark One, and noticed that his clothes were wrinkled, unclean, as if he had been wearing them for several days. His head was bowed, his shoulders shaking. Was he crying? As if in response to Richard's silent question, the Dark One raised his head, and Richard could plainly see that the green eyes, once sparkling with joy and amusement, now glistened with tears.

The tightness in Richard's chest had returned, threefold the pain he had felt the first day the Blond and the Dark One had failed to turn up for their noontime encounter. Richard studied the Dark One more closely, and saw that his hands were not still. He seemed to be turning something over and over in his palms, and only after closer scrutiny did Richard notice it was a ring – a ring that matched the Dark One's own – a ring that used to sit on the perfectly manicured hand that Richard last saw holding out a piece of paper to the Dark One.

Richard suddenly, and with a clarity that had years ago escaped him, felt the entire experience of watching the relationship between these two men blossom and grow and, as it sadly seemed, end. Had he witnessed the final act?

Suddenly, Richard knew without a doubt that he had to help the Dark One. Through the window, he saw the Dark One stand, never taking his eyes of the ring that lay in the palm of his bare hand. Slowly, he turned and looked south, then east, then north. Again, his eyes drifted to the ring in his hand, as if it were not a ring but a compass to help guide the Dark One's way.

He then looked directly at Richard's apartment building, which lay to the west of where the Dark One stood.

The Dark One pulled a silver chain from his pocket, and slipped it through the Blond's ring. Grasping both ends, he held it aloft, looking at the ring, and smiled.

Smiling? That seemed odd. He watched the Dark One speak, and after years of watching their encounters, Richard could finally make out the words that were being said.

"I'll see you soon, my love."

He fastened the chain around his neck, and tucked the ring underneath his shirt.

Richard was decided, and oddly, charged with an energy that he had not felt since he was a much younger man. He walked determinedly through the apartment, startling the caretaker who was enraptured by the television in the living room. He could hear her protests behind him as he threw open the door, and began down the stairs. Had there always been this many stairs? Finally, with gravity's help, he reached the bottom and stepped through the front doors and out onto the street.

His skin tensed in the sudden chill, but without a pause, he strode across the street and into the forgotten park, wedged between two taller buildings on either side.

His breathing became labored, and Richard's eyes searched the park, but the Dark One was gone. Gone also was the bench, a patch of bare ground where it once stood. The hedge had been cut down, only the twisted tops of the roots remaining above ground. Richard quickly looked over his shoulder to make sure that his apartment building was still there, and it was, wedged between two taller buildings, much like the park.

What was happening? Did he imagine it all? He thrashed around the park, searching for something, anything that would make the time he spent watching this wretched piece of earth every day worthwhile. Where were the phantoms who joined him nearly each and every day for lunch? Where was their anger and their joy, laid bare for Richard to witness as he shared each noon meal with them?

Was it all a fantasy?

Richard saw the caretaker rushing across the street, and he knew that soon an ambulance would follow. He lifted his eyes to his third-story window, knowing he would never see the inside of his apartment again.

He was shocked to realize that he did not care about that fact. The Blond and the Dark One had breathed life into his existence, portraying only for him those things from which he had always run in fear – that love, that passion, that forgiveness, that temperance, that perfect balance. He would never know these things, but thanks to the unwitting efforts of these two men, now he at least knew of them.

The caretaker reached him, and while he felt her heavy arm around his shoulders, and while he heard her barking instructions into a portable phone, he had already taken leave of this scene.

The ambulance did come, and it did whisk him away, and he never saw his apartment again. During those last few weeks of his life, Richard never told the story of the Blond and the Dark One to a single person, and the caretaker who had chased him into the park treated his hysterical pleading on that day as she would the ramblings of any other demented patient.

Three weeks later, Richard Charles McGlommer, IV left this life. And while there would not be another Richard Charles McGlommer to follow in his footsteps, there was a forgotten park in the city, which used to have a hedge and a bench. And if he had ever gotten close enough to look, Richard would have seen a small plaque on the top rail of the bench, bearing this inscription, long since faded…

> HERE, ONE DAY,
> A MAN ASKED ANOTHER MAN TO MARRY HIM,
> FAULTS AND ALL.
> THE STATE WOULD NOT ALLOW IT,
> AND THEIR FAMILIES WOULD NOT ACCEPT IT, BUT,
> HE SAID,
> WITHOUT HESITATION,
> ## YES.

CHAIRS

For the first time in my life, I peer over my shoulder and gaze at the dingy linoleum far below. My tiny legs stick out perpendicular to my body, my knees resting flat on the seat. A woman looms over me, her watchful eyes trained constantly on me. She is familiar; in fact, she is the only one I remember in my existence. She has an oddly-shaped device in her hand, with a thick, green syrupy substance dripping from its flat, rounded tip. Without warning, she jabs the device into my mouth, and as I part my lips to scream, swallowing is involuntary. My tiny stomach is slightly satisfied, yet this contentment does not extend to my tongue. Although I am less than one year of age, I can say with complete confidence that I shall, always and forever, hate the taste of peas—strained, or otherwise prepared.

The chairs in this room are chaotically colorful; each painted a different color, and no two are alike in shade. I choose the red one, close to the tall woman with dark skin and short black hair. I do not know much about her, but she's the biggest thing here, and it pays to have powerful friends. A boy beside me tells me to give him the red chair, that he "called it."

"What did you call it?" I ask. The Big Lady laughs. A little later, when I return from a trip to the Big Shiny Bathroom the Size of Half My House, the boy is sitting in the red chair, satisfied, and smiling a cartoonishly large smile. Suddenly, everything I see is tinted with a touch of red. Seconds later, the boy is on the floor, his smile gone, and his face swelling.

The chairs in Prince Sea Pal's office are much larger than those in the room with the Big Lady. For a second, I think that my grandmother is sitting behind the small wall. Happily, I call out her name, but when she turns around, I know immediately this is not my grandmother. My grandmother has more silver in her hair, and doesn't look like she was sucking on a lemon. There is an odd device on the wall; it looks like a large thermometer, complete with the round part and the red "blood" that all thermometers have, but it has a beak like a bird at the top, and is wearing a silly hat. It keeps dipping its beak into a cup of water, but the water inside the "bird" never goes up, and the water inside of the glass never goes down. An big man comes up to speak to me. He says he's the Prince Sea Pal. He doesn't look like a prince. As he leads me to his office, I wonder if his chair is a throne.

The chairs now have small tables attached. It's a good thing; with English and Modern European History back-to-back, not to mention two teachers notorious for their essay questions, I need all the table space I can get. The history teacher is the more brutal of the two. Her tests consist of two components: one essay question and one admonishment: "Describe the effect of the French Revolution on the rest of Europe from a political and fiscal standpoint," and "If you can't impress me, you should, at least, entertain me." Putting pen to paper, I wonder if the uncomfortable nature of these chairs is a measure to prevent students from sleeping. The material we study is enough to keep me awake, but some of the other students doze off occasionally, material and mechanical preventions be damned.

I am surrounded by chairs, with tables scattered amongst them, all in the same rich wood and green leather upholstery, all with the lingering scent of Murphy's Oil Soap that had been laboriously applied by the closers last night. I survey the floor, ensuring that all is in order before I open the doors for the lunch crowd. Soon, all these chairs will be full, and then they will become hazards for the white and black clad dancers who perform the strange ballet among the onlookers rather than before them. The audience is a rude one, but it is not their fault; to them the dancers are merely set dressing as they broker deals, reaffirm acquaintances, and consume fuel for the rest of the day. Just over an hour later, most of these chairs will be empty, only the exhausted dancers, resting and preparing for the evening performance, remain. Tonight's show will last much longer than an hour.

This chair is stolen.

Well, not exactly stolen. "Appropriated" is a much better word. It was liberated from an executive's old office down the hall that has sat vacant since the former occupant, the company's Vice-President of Something Important, retired or died or transferred or quit. This chair is much better than the one deemed appropriate for my station, but being the Golden Boy has its perks. My boss, the Chief Executive Something has been quite forthcoming with his professional advice and guidance, and, as a result, I have risen quickly to now sit immediately outside his office, his protection from the rest of the world. From my newly-appropriated throne, I dispense access to my executive with the fairness and propriety of Elizabeth the First. Cross me, and while I will continue to be fair and proper, I will make sure everyone hears about your transgression in a matter of hours.

There are only two chairs at this table, tucked on top of dingy tile. The eyes that stare back at me are deep brown, peeking out from under a mop of reddish-brown hair. Few words are spoken, as neither of us prefer mornings. We learned early enough in our relationship to just sit quietly and wait for the magic of caffeine to run its course. He has the day off, and is bugging me to not "go to work" today, even though I now work out of our home. I mutter something about being reliable and responsible, and he gets up to get us more coffee. Suddenly, arms encircle my waist and his lips descend on the lobe of my ear, and while I cannot, for the life of me, remember what I was thinking, I know one thing is for sure: I will be late "to work," if I make it at all.

There are rows of chairs here, each identical with a gold bambooesque frame and white padded seats. By eschewing tradition for beliefs that we both hold dear, we allow our families, natural and chosen, to mingle freely across the aisle. I pace nervously amongst them offering greetings and accepting congratulations. Time seems to be set on fast-forward, for out of nowhere the music swells, and I turn. Under the awning he stands, brown eyes twinkling the same way they did when we first met. All of a sudden, I need to sit down.

Chairs in a doctor's waiting room are designed more for efficiency rather than comfort, and it really should be the other way around. We are here again, the third visit in as many days, this time to hear news that cannot be given over the phone. The door cracks and the nurse, once an acquaintance but now a friend, smiles a small smile and waves us back. She could have stuck her tongue out and waggled it at us in the silliest manner possible, but even that would not have lifted the sadness from her eyes.

This chair is designed for comfort, though the supplest leather and a frame hand-crafted to match my own would not have relieved me of the despair that I feel. He sits next to me, sometimes joined by others, sometimes alone. The fluids that drip into the port in my chest do not burn, nor do they make me cold. We pass the time with magazines, cards, and a laptop computer, my desperate attachment to my work an insufficient touchstone to the real world. He remains strong, but every now and then he excuses himself to use the facilities. I pretend not to see the tear tracks on his cheeks when he returns.

This chair is more complicated than any one I have ever known. Its large wheels are cumbersome as they roll down the cobbled street of the coastal Georgia town where we spend many a night. I can no longer smell the salt on the air, and the chill off the ocean simply blends in to the cold grip that now relentlessly possesses my entire body. He dutifully rolls me into our favorite haunts, but the lobster is less succulent, the crab less sweet, the wine less robust. This chair ensures our wait will be short, and our service will be impeccable. I would gladly give up this chair in order to be able to stand for an hour at the bar and wonder where our waiter had gone.

These chairs are somber, black padding on black metal. I move amongst them, through them, unable to take a seat. I see him in the front row, his once broad shoulders small and hunched. The woman who once fed me in the high chair walks up, and once again, she has a crying baby in her arms, though this one possesses the body of a man. I whip forward, my heart only wanting to comfort them, but I cannot. More people fill the room, but to me, only those two exist, an island amongst this black sea, their pain a physical quality now possessed by their bodies. The blackness fades in, and I wonder if there are chairs where I am going.

THE BALLAD OF
BIG RED

DESPITE BEING THE CAPITAL OF THE COMMONWEALTH of Pennsylvania, the City of Harrisburg maintains a distinct "small-town" vibe – a relatively limited downtown area giving way to a gently rolling landscape covered by single family houses and single-building businesses, growing sparser the further away from the Susquehanna River one travels. While the town, in the esoteric sense, is often described as "warm and cozy," the same cannot be said about the current climatic conditions.

It isn't just cold; it's damn near freezing.

The cab drops me off at the corner of Second and Forster, a simple half-block or so from my destination. I discovered The Brownstone Lounge on one of my many trips to Harrisburg, home of my employer's corporate headquarters, and I have become quite a frequent guest, striking up a friendship or two with some of the locals. Even the owner of the bar knows who I am, although it seems the irony of calling me "A.A." (short for "Adam from Atlanta") in a bar is completely lost on her.

I pull my gray wool coat tight to my body, and start
the uphill climb, which tonight seems much longer than
normal. Night is falling around me in earnest, and the only
source of light is the ambient glow from the gas station
on the corner, and the streetlights which line the nearly
deserted avenue. I attempt to quicken my step, but the gale
blowing in my face slows my progress to a crawling pace.

At last, I step through the glass door, make an
obligatory half-turn to the left through another archway,
and find myself at the short end of a shotgun bar. The
lights are lowered, the televisions providing more
illumination than the lamps. Men, and a couple of women,
sit hunched over drinks, and the few booths opposite the
bar are already full. Fortune seems to be with me, however,
and I slip, unnoticed, into a seat halfway down the bar.

The bartender, a cartoonish grin on his face, takes my
order, and soon a perfect martini, so "dirty" it can only be
described as "outright filthy," is placed on the bar before
me, standing out in the sea of draft beer and cocktails in
tall glasses. Pennsylvania, unlike my repressed home of
Georgia, still offers a true happy hour, and apparently "two
for one" includes combining two drinks in the same glass.

Another reason I do not totally despise the frequent
trips north is the fact that smoking has not been completely
banned from public buildings. I slip a pack of Marlboros
out of my coat pocket, and set them on the bar before me,
but not before taking one, lighting it, and drawing deep on
the smoldering tobacco. The smoke hits my lungs like a
hammer, and for a moment I am light headed; it had been
a long day of meeting after meeting, and I had not had
that many chances to slip unnoticed to the back parking
lot of the office to indulge in a habit that I simultaneously
cherish and despise. It is difficult to unobtrusively adorn a

full-length coat, scarf, hat and gloves while one's peers are simply stepping to the restroom.

I make idle chatter with the bartender; I do likewise with the gentlemen on my left and on my right. We discuss my origins, what has been going on in local affairs, our views on national affairs, and where on the beauty scale everyone rates—everyone within eyesight but out of earshot, of course. While the superficial queens of Atlanta may very well win if judged on looks alone, the men here exude friendliness with an ease that instantly elevates their attractiveness, nearly nullifying the nelly nancies of my hometown.

"WELL, I DEE-CLARE!"

Although I know it is unlikely, I could swear the room has gone as silent as the grave. This is my third straight week in Harrisburg, and I have grown so accustomed to the local dialect, that the shock of the Tennessee mountain drawl echoes over the din from the bar like a shot from a Confederate cannon.

The corners of my lips twitch upward in a small smile. That voice can only mean one thing – the rednecks have come to roost.

Without so much as a glance over my shoulder, I already know who is standing in the doorway. Michael Charles, or simply M.C.—one of the locals with whom I have formed a fast and oddly, deep friendship—has apparently received all my texts, despite his proven inability to reply to them. The man to my right looks over his shoulder, and then quickly collects his drink, suddenly remembering that he needs to speak to someone at another part of the bar. M.C. watches him go with a look of smug approval on his face, nods once, and then plants himself next to me.

"Sorry I couldn't text you back, Julia," he greets, air-kissing my cheek. M.C. insists on calling me Julia due to our mutual love of the 1980's television show *Designing Women*. It does not bother me; I get to call him Suzanne. "Broom Hilda has been in the office all week and has been standing on my very last nerve."

"No worries," I reply, signaling the bartender for another martini.

After a moment's thought, I add a couple of shots to the order. I had chosen to take a cab tonight for the explicit purpose of not having to drive. Besides, M.C. and I are much more entertaining when we're sufficiently intoxicated. Just ask us; we'll tell you.

"So, my darlin'," he drawls. "Tell me, what news of the South?"

"Well, I honestly don't know. Lately, I just pay taxes there. It seems like I live in the Delta SkyClub." This is complete bullshit as I usually fly USAir. "I did get a call from my cousin the other day. Apparently, it snowed down there about two days before, and she was wondering if I had heat and hot water."

A universal truth suddenly struck me: outside of a blizzard big enough to make the national news, snow does not last for three days in Atlanta.

"She's full of it," he declares, "snow doesn't last for three days down there." He holds his shot glass up so we can toast before downing the contents. I mirror his motions, our glasses touching, the telltale clink audible only to the two of us. As we toss their contents back, the jukebox, silent up until now, suddenly and forcefully announces its presence. M.C. begins to choke, but recovers, and he seems personally affronted by the current selection, although neither of us had seen the perpetrator who made this choice.

It turns out that the lack of such trivial details would never stop M.C. from making sure the self-appointed DJ, whomever it was, knew he had chosen poorly.

"ALL RIGHT! WHICH ONE OF YOU BITCHES PICKED CHER? HOW CLICHÉ!"

"Um, M.C.?"

"Yes, darlin'?"

"Aren't we pretty much clichés ourself?" I ask, realizing my error. "I mean… ourselves?"

"Oh, my dear," he says as he pats my hand, "don't put on airs. Despite your cosmopolitan address, you and I both know your family's necks are just as red as mine."

I laugh heartily, and order us another round. It was going to be a good night. M.C. jumps up from his chair, and promptly relieves me of four dollar bills. I raise an eyebrow, and he air-kisses my cheek again. "I'm going to go fix the music," he whispers conspiratorially in my ear, "and when I get back, you can finish that story you started about your crazy relative. What did you call her? Double Mint?"

"Big Red."

"Whatever," says M.C., already turning to walk the scant seven steps to the jukebox. I pick up my glass, but almost drop it when he yells, "HEY! YA'LL GOT 'DUELIN' BANJOS' ON THIS THING?"

Big Red earned her nickname neither by being obese nor due to an overabundance of mammary tissue. She got her name because of her hair.

Being a dyed-in-the-wool Southerner, Big Red held fast to the rule that "the higher the hair, the closer to God." She used so much Aqua Net that it was a miracle that she was not personally credited with the gigantic hole in the ozone layer. Add to the mix a bottle of drugstore-bought Crimson Cinnamon hair dye, and you had a tried and true redneck beauty queen, complete with everything but the beauty.

Born and raised in the rural ruin of Wetsawannakah County, Alabama, Big Red enjoyed her childhood and adolescence, and while life did not resemble a Norman Rockwell painting or an episode of The Donna Reed Show, it was not horrible. She graduated high school in the allotted number of years, and that is where the wheels began to come off the wagon.

While members of my family may have succumbed to wanderlust in their early twenties, we always managed to return to live within driving distance of our relations. Big Red was no different – after a stint at college in Oregon, she beat a quick path back to the Bible Belt, complete with a legal separation in one hand and a toddler in the other.

Honestly, all she was missing was the housecoat and curlers.

She quickly divorced, and set about finding her next victim—er, husband. Widespread use of the Internet was in its infancy, and most homes still used programs like America Online to connect them instantly with liars and perverts everywhere. Big Red took things slowly at first—only a *couple of hours per day—but soon, the anonymous mating dance in cyberspace seemed to consume her entire life.*

She stopped looking for a job, and found herself living in a tiny room in her mother Priscilla's basement. Her father, my uncle, had passed away nearly twenty years before, and since then it had just been the two girls. Big Red's daughter Melody completed the trio, having narrowly avoided the name Little Red by inheriting her father's Teutonic features, specifically the blonde hair.

"How does an Alabammy redneck have an Aryan baby?" M.C. asks, drawing long stares from those who had, during my tale, moved to sit near us. What little momentum I had built disappears, which is standard with any conversation in which M.C. is taking part. He has the singular talent of being able to stop a dialogue dead in its tracks, usually with the force of a rather large hand grenade, or small land mine. Happy Hour has long left us, and we are coming into the time of night where waiters and other restaurant employees began to trickle into the bar. My people.

"She wasn't Aryan; she didn't have blue eyes," I snap. "Now, your holiness, if you don't mind?"

"But what color was Big Red's hair?" M.C. asks, his eyes glassy and his cheeks flush.

"Red. Her hair was big and red. Are you even listening?" My patience is suddenly wearing thin. The bartender slips another martini in front of me, his silent proffer enough to start settling my nerves. "Big Red goes to college, gets married, has a baby, gets divorced, starts looking for men on the Internet. Are you all caught up now?"

"An Aryan baby…" M.C. wants to dwell on this point, apparently.

"If I say yes, can I keep going with the story?" God, I'm a smart-ass.

"Yes, dear, you may," answers M.C., granting his permission with all the grace of a royal. He is truly a monarch in his own mind.

Big Red's men would come and go; no one in the family really saw much of them, if they saw anything at all. Honestly, no one really paid them that much attention. If they were worth knowing, they would stick around for longer than a weekend.

Everything changed, however, one Sunday night at the home of my grandparents, William and Charity Lawrence. She was in her late sixties, he in his early eighties. William, whom we all called "Pop," had already begun the long, slow decline toward death, in which the men in my family are often known to malinger for up to a decade. He spent much of his time just sitting in a chair, staring into space. He called it "waiting for the boneyard." I firmly believed that my grandmother, whom we all called "Charity" at her insistence, was keeping him alive out of sheer will, as Pop was often quick to quip that he read the obituaries daily in order to see if his name was listed among the deceased. I have never witnessed a stronger love between two people, and it was this kind of love to which all their descendants aspired, each with varying degrees of success.

I parked my old, run-down Honda Accord in the driveway of the single-story brick ranch house right behind my father's shiny black Jeep Grand Cherokee. Mother and Dad were just getting out of the car, so we walked in together. A white Toyota Highlander told me that my kid brother Carl, most likely with his fiancée Denise, had already arrived, and I could just hear the deep, throaty roar of the old Chevy Nova that my father's brother Brad had restored and was now driving down the street toward my grandparents' house. Relatives continued to arrive in this fashion, and before long, the house was nearly bursting with bodies. We did not even notice that Big Red had walked through the door, at least not until she spoke loudly enough to drown out all other conversation.

"Y'ain't gonna believe this; I met a new guy!" she yelled to Denise, who was all of a foot away from her. "He's the cutest thing ever!"

"Really?" Denise replied, genuinely interested. "Who is he? What's does he do?"

"His name's Jeffrey, and he's in the Army." Now Big Red was smug. "He's in Afghanistan."

At this point, we as a group forwent the pretense of chatting among ourselves, and turned our attention as a whole to Big Red. The Un-Beauty Queen had finally found her throne, and we were her courtiers. "Well, he's stationed in Columbus, but he's deployed right now."

"That's so brave," Denise purrs. We have always been a military family. Pop was in the Army during World War II, along with several of his brothers. I myself did a stint in the Air Force, and a couple of my cousins were even on active duty in the Navy. Regarding potential spouses, military service was an immediate advantage as far as we were concerned. "What part of the Army? I had an ex once who was infantry."

"He can't talkaboutit; it's...well, it's Classified Top Secret," responded Big Red, trying to conceal a smile and failing spectacularly. "We don't talk about that stuff, though. It's bad enough he has to be over there inthethickofit." Big Red's rural speech had a tendency to run idiomatic expressions together into a single word. "We talkabout... the future."

The word "future" hung in the air like an unexploded bomb. Short engagements were taboo in our family; Carl had dated Denise for almost eight years before he finally proposed about six months ago. It would be another nine months before their wedding. In fact, the shortest family engagement on record, six weeks, belonged to my own parents, but anyone who saw them together knew that they were meant for each other. We all looked to Denise in order to determine how to proceed.

"What does he look like?" Denise asked, changing subjects deftly. Denise was easily the most social among us, and no one rose to her level without having learned a thing or two about verbal manipulation. "I mean... is he your typical soldier—crew-cut hair and boring clothes, or is he a little more... interesting?"

Conversation continued in this vein until we had covered all the relevant information about Big Red's new boyfriend—the mysterious Jeffrey. By the time we sat down *to dinner, we already knew that, despite being in the Army and deployed to Afghanistan, he managed to sit behind a computer for 12 hours a day. Big Red had never seen him or spoken to him, but had exchanged pictures. Daily instant messenger sessions normally lasted six to eight hours.*

As often followed a carbohydrate-laden meal at my grandparents' house, the time after dinner was spent sitting in chairs and chatting, or in my father's case, spending half of the time sleeping, and the other half denying that he had dozed off at all. I chose to leave almost directly after dinner, and as I pulled away from the house and turned my car toward an antique store along a slightly more populated stretch of Georgia Highway 138, any thought of my cousin's new beau fled my mind.

"Antiquing on a Sunday afternoon?" M.C. is incredulous. "What was so damn important that you couldn't stay there and get the goods on this guy? An early brunch the next day? A black-tie gala to support a near-unknown cause? I swear you Atlanta queens have your priorities way out of whack."

"Whatever," I grumble. I had stopped drinking half an hour before, and am beginning to rethink that decision. It is nearly midnight, and I am wondering why I am still here at the bar, staring into the empty space where my last martini stood. My thoughts begin to wander, and I almost do not hear the voice from my left.

"So what happened?" the voice asks. Instinctively, I turn toward my right, to where M.C. sits, his eyelids starting to slip shut. Confused, I turn the other direction, and I am shocked to see an even larger crowd of attentive faces turned toward me, a couple of them nodding encouragingly. A bearded face that I have never met, apparently the self-elected spokesperson of the group, pushes me to continue my story.

"What happened next?"

"My brother got married."

The day that Carl Winstead Lawrence married Denise DeLangley dawned cool and clear. As with any Georgia Saturday in mid-September, this meant nothing by the scheduled time of the wedding at three in the afternoon. When the music swelled and my soon-to-be sister-in-law took her first steps down the aisle toward her betrothed, I had nearly sweat through my rented tuxedo. I could see Melody, barely seven years old, standing among the bridesmaids that she had preceded, scattering rose petals as she went. Denise did not come from a large family, and had so completely integrated into ours that the inclusion of Big Red's daughter in the wedding party was practically a forgone conclusion. Besides, my cousin Chuck would have looked silly in a frilly dress.

As with any properly planned Southern wedding, the mother of the flower girl sits on the front row, ready to remove the youngster from the dais should she show the slightest hint that she may become disruptive. Melody's behavior was as sweet as a song, which left Big Red on the front pew, alone. By sheer coincidence, my favorite date for all functions—my best friend Alanna—was seated right behind her, and about halfway through the vows, she did something that, at first, confused me.

She started to raise her hand.

I knew that she did not have a question. I knew that she was not trying to interrupt the service. As an added layer of control, my new sister-in-law insisted that the minister skip over the "Should anyone feel that these two should not be joined" section for reasons that remain, to this day, her own.

No, Alanna was making plucking motions behind Big Red's hair, which had been swept up, twisted, and secured in place with a pair of chopsticks. I had known Alanna long enough to know that she would never do something as gauche as to disrupt a wedding, but for the life of me I could not figure out what she was doing. I dragged my attention back to the happy couple, putting the entire thing out of my mind for the time being.

In fact, I did not think of it again until I was standing patiently in the aisle waiting for my mother to take my arm, and I glanced over to where Alanna was now pointing directly at the back of Big Red's head. The stunning realization hit me instantly now that I could see what Alanna had been trying to show me since three minutes into the wedding. The chopsticks that Big Red had chosen to hold up her hair were not the black, lacquered, hand-painted kind that one normally uses for such a hairstyle. They were the plain bamboo ones that you get tucked into Kung Pao Chicken when you pick up your order from the Grand China Buffet, and must break apart before using them.

For a bar at one in the morning, the Brownstone is as silent as a morgue. The only patrons remaining have gathered around me, and are listening with rapt attention. M.C. has shaken off his slumber, and pipes up for the first time in half an hour.

"You have got to be kidding me."

"I assure you, I am not," I respond. "Chinese. Takeaway. Chopsticks."

"Did they at least match her dress?" asks another patron, clearly missing the point.

"Not really. But what accoutrement would you recommend for a strapless maroon prom dress?" I am starting to get a tad touchy; it is late and I am notorious for burning the candle at both ends when I travel for work.

"Anyway, we had just gotten to the wedding pictures..."

The photographer was busy posing smaller groups of the wedding party, first the bride and groom, then several sections and subsections of the wedding party. It was when we tried to get one of these larger groups together did we realized that someone was missing.

The flower girl was nowhere to be found.

Now, being only seven years old, Melody was incapable of driving away on her own. Several well-meaning family members were dispatched to various points of the church to see if she was in any of the usually suspected places: the ladies' room, the playground, the vestry, the balcony. I even suggested that she was with the bridesmaids getting drunk in the changing room, a suggestion that my mother promptly informed me was "not appropriate" and I had better "watch it."

The woman has never appreciated my sense of humor.

As my mother was berating me, Priscilla, Melody's grandmother, happened to wander into the church sanctuary, casually speaking to someone I did not recognize. Noticing my lack of attention, my mother turned around and stalked, stiff backed and stone faced, over to where Priscilla stood. She drew to within inches of her, and a few words were exchanged. Obviously unhappy with what she heard, my mother turned on a single heel and marched back down to where we were all standing, but spoke to no one.

"Does Aunt Prissy know where Melody is?" I asked.

"It seems that rushing home to talk to her boyfriend online was more important to my niece than having the entire bridal party in a single photograph."

I was stunned. I had heard through various people that Big Red's "relationship" with Jeffrey was beginning to border on the obsessive, but I had dismissed most of those rumors as just the embellishments of an aunt who liked to be the center of attention. But the idea of snatching up her daughter, the flower girl, and leaving the church so she could drive almost an hour away to chat online with a man who, after a year and a half, had not even bothered to pick up the phone? I've always been a proponent of fighting for love and all that, but to risk my mother's legendary wrath with such a stunt was just stupid. I would have invested in a laptop. In the long *run, it would have been cheaper than the emergency room bill Big Red would face had my mother caught up to her.*

After the wedding, we all returned to our lives, and little more was said on the subject. Jeffery became somewhat of a joke among the family, mostly owing to that for the almost two years that they had been "together," Big Red had never met him. She had never seen him. Instead, in a tale reminiscent of Victorian England, they would merely exchange letters, confessing their undying love for each other, but never once breathing the same air.

Isn't the whole point to actually be with the person with whom you are in love?

While I had always been one of the largest skeptics, even the most gullible members of my family began to wonder if Jeffrey was real, or if Big Red was being tragically manipulated by some cyber-sociopath who wanted nothing more than to toy with the emotions of a woman who, despite her best intentions, had managed to become trapped in his web of deception and lies.

My brother and his new wife settled into a house not far from where I lived, and while they were not frequent guests, they did occasionally visit. In the beginning, Denise remained somewhat close with Big Red, despite the flower girl debacle, but they drifted further apart as Denise graduated from nursing school and began to work at Piedmont Hospital, and Big Red remained... well, Big Red.

Unfortunately, Pop's health began to really fail around this time. Despite Charity's conviction that he should live forever, it soon became apparent that the end was truly near. Charity began to host every single holiday celebration possible at their home, as if she could cram another decade of life into a single year.

No one begrudged her a single bit.

I can't remember if it was Easter, or Mother's Day, or a combination Arbor Day/Twelfth Night celebration, but once again, we were all gathered in the single-story brick house outside of Atlanta. Pop had always been the chef of the family, and it seemed that all the family tales revolved around a meal.

When I arrived (late) for this gathering, the meal was already in full swing. Dutifully, I greeted whom I needed to (my parents, Charity, and Pop), accepted a plate full of food pressed into my hand by my grandmother, and took a seat next to my mother at the dining room table. Random cousins were also at the table, and at the other end, huddled in conversation, were Denise and Big Red.

"Honey, I don't think that's what happened..." said Denise, almost pleading.

"But that's what the doctor said. He said he had a stroke," wailed Big Red, louder than I was sure she had intended.

The word "stroke" stopped all conversation cold. Pop's hardening arteries had put him at risk when he was still in his early forties, but with two angioplasties and an open-heart surgery under his belt, his chance of a stroke had increased a hundred fold.

"Even if he did have a stroke, he stands a better chance of recovery," Denise said soothingly, trying to comfort the near-hysterical Big Red. "The younger you are, the better off you are. Didn't you say that he said he was only twenty-three?"

I caught my sister-in-law's turn of phrase like an easy grounder hit by a four-year-old. Even the always-accepting Denise was starting to have her doubts.

Before Big Red could answer, however, my mother chose to enter the discussion, the memory of my brother's wedding apparently still somewhat fresh in her mind.

"How can you tell he had a stroke? Does he slur his e-mails?"

It is now after two, and the bar is alive with raucous laughter. My mother had always been known for her stiletto-sharp wit, but that one phrase has managed to live in infamy for almost ten years. From the rolling wall of laughter, questions begin to jump out at me:

"Did Jeffrey die?"

"Did she really say that?"

"I can't believe your mother said that. I mean... Why did she say that?"

I am in the middle of a sip of coffee that had been brewed half an hour earlier, the bartender determined to stay open until the tale was told. Fortunately, M.C. chooses that moment to enter the fray.

"Yankees don't know a damn thing," he states, plainly. "You see, in the South, we're a bit more... direct."

I stifle a yawn, and realize that it's time for me to bring this tale to an end. The eyes trained on me are bleary, and I have to be at the office at some ungodly hour tomorrow; one of the downfalls of traveling with my boss, Mr. Early-

Riser. The only offset, however, is that he never argues with me when I want to stop by Starbucks each and every morning we are in town. The coffee at the office is just pure crap.

It was only another couple of months before we were all gathered at Pop and Charity's house for Flag Day. Or Veteran's Day. Or Thursday. Once again, Big Red was sitting center stage, but instead of wailing and gnashing teeth, she was feeling quite pleased with herself.

"I talked to Jeffery before we came over here today," she said proudly. Every other person in the room looked at each other with the same question in their mind: Talked? As in verbal communication?

"He's doing so well in his rehabilitation," she continued, undaunted by the disbelieving faces around her. "When we talk to each other, I have to help him learn his words again. It's a side effect of the stroke."

At that point, even I was started to get confused at what we were being told. I glanced over to Denise, who was staring at a book pretending to read, for no other reason than as the sole medical caregiver in the family, she would be called upon to validate Big Red's claims. Now, it seemed that she wanted nothing to do with the situation at all. I honestly could not blame her.

"First," Big Red explained, falsely assuming that anyone in the room gave a damn, "I type the word see-ay-arruh. Then I send 'im a picture of a car so he knows

whatitlookslike. Then I type tee-arruh-eee-eee. And then I send 'im a picture of a tree. It takes me so so so long to find these pictures online b'fore our talks; I almost don't have time to talk to him at all."

I was pondering whether or not reduced conversation time with Jeffrey was a bad thing when I heard my mother's voice once again.

"So let me get this straight," she scoffed. "He doesn't know what a car is, and he doesn't know what a tree is. But he knows how to operate a computer and get on the goddamn Internet?"

Silence landed on the room like an oversized wet blanket dropped from a mile in the air. No one knew what to do next, and I could see the tears starting to well in Big Red's eyes. I grabbed my keys, kissed Charity on the cheek, and slipped out the door. I disapproved of neither my mother's words, nor Big Red's choices for that matter. I did know that this saga had taken up as much time in my life as I was going to allow, and besides, the used bookstore in the next town had a set of Queen Anne chairs over which I wanted to haggle.

Three months later, I got a call from my Favorite Aunt. The day before, Big Red had received an e-mail from someone she did not know that stated quite simply that Jeffrey had succumbed to his injuries and died. There would be no further communication, and the message did not give any details of a memorial service, obituary or funeral. My aunt wanted to know if I could look into the e-mail message and determine from whence it came. She forwarded the e-mail, but I quickly called her back and told her simply that there was nothing I could do.

At the time of his alleged death, "Jeffrey" and Big Red were together for two years, six months, and five days. And while Jeffery may have been an impostor, and while he may have only been playing with her emotions, there was a woman, who lived in her mother's basement, who had a daughter, and to whom that relationship was real, to whom the thought of Jeffery made her light up like a Christmas tree.

A Christmas tree topped with a star made out of Chinese takeaway chopsticks.

The patrons of the bar, their taste for someone else's tragedy sated, begin to make their way home. As we have long since sobered up, M.C. and I jump in his aged Ford Explorer, and ride in silence up U.S. 22 toward my hotel. After we pull into the parking lot, he turns to me and asks a question that has obviously been on his mind for quite some time.

"What happened next?"

"What do you mean?"

"You know what I mean, Julia," M.C. presses. "What happened to Big Red after Mister Man died?"

"Well, she moved on. She got a job, a good job, and then she got a man, a good man, a real man. She brings him around on holidays, although I think she does it just to make sure we all can see that he's real." I am shocked to hear the pride in my own voice as I speak of my cousin. I have yet to be so lucky in love. "They got engaged this past summer."

"Good for her. Now go to bed. Maybe you can get just enough beauty sleep to take care of the three pimples on your face that you are pretending are not there." He air kisses me again, and soon I'm back in the hotel, in my room, my laptop open on the dresser next to my briefcase.

I take a thumb drive out of a side pocket of my bag, and slip it into the USB port on my laptop. A window pops open on the screen, where a single PDF document is shown. I open up a copy of the e-mail my Favorite Aunt sent me years ago, and look at the routing information that I had gathered the very day that she sent it to me, before I decided to tell her that I could find nothing at all. I chuckle at the whole thing before I yank the drive out of the laptop, toss it back into my bag, and begin to get ready for bed, the location of the man known to us simply as "Jeffery" locked safely away in a file on a thumb drive in a briefcase in a hotel in the big small town of Harrisburg, Pennsylvania, capital of the Commonwealth.

THE
SANCTUARY
OF THE MIND

"I WILL KILL YOU ONE DAY," Jonathan said to his girlfriend, Melissa. "There is nothing you can do to stop it."

It felt like these were the last words that he would ever say to her. She packed the few things that she could find in the moment, and fled their home in the space of a mere ten minutes.

Once again, Jonathan found himself alone. Once again, he found himself to be the only one to blame.

This last episode was one of the worst he could remember; not that he could remember much of anything. In fact, that he possessed any memory of it at all could only mean one thing.

It had been exceptionally horrific.

For nearly an hour, he sat, without moving, on the edge of the torn and broken sofa that dominated the tiny living room. He stared straight ahead, but did not see the television lying face-down and broken on the floor. He did not see the splintered remnants of picture frames which formerly held the now-torn images of family members and friends.

Instead, he was looking inward.

To an outside observer, Jonathan appeared as carved stone, his vitality belied by the ever so slight expansion and contraction of his chest as he drew rapid, shallow breaths.

"Why?"

The question was exhaled rather than spoken, for there was no one to hear him anymore. Yet Jonathan was not shocked when he heard the response.

"*You know why*," answered the Voice.

Again, he lapsed into silence, slipping deeper and deeper into his own consciousness until the tattered remains of his once-shared home dissolved around him. He appeared, as he did so many times before, on the path that only he could see.

As he did so often before, he wanted nothing more than to return to the real world – the world that everyone could see – and leave this dreadful place.

A simple path led through a thick forest, but Jonathan could already see the light pulsing through the cracks between the trees. The light was so bright that the details of the trees and flora were lost to silhouette. In the background he could hear the strangely musical but discordant cacophony, the sound growing louder and louder the closer he moved to what was, always, his destination.

The Carnival of the Damned.

Jonathan did not travel this path voluntarily. Nay, he was pulled forward, and while he no longer offered any resistance, he did not assist his tormentor in hastening his step. Instead, he cast around for a lifeline that he could use to pull himself out of this nightmare.

But now, his lifeline was gone.

He had not wanted to kill Melissa; she had been the most patient, the most caring, the most… understanding of all. The intensity of their physical connection was outweighed by their emotional bond the way a feather is outweighed by a mountain of lead. Every time she was near, he swore he could feel his heartbeat lining up with hers, his breath moving in time with her breath. He could hear her thoughts – actually hear them – and she claimed to be able to hear his, although he knew that she was lying. He forgave her this one flaw.

Jonathan was *special*; everyone who had ever cared about him had assured him of this fact.

"I told you that you couldn't trust her," said the Voice. *"Look—she's already left. Barely lasted a year, that one did. That's why you have to stay in here. It's the only way you won't get hurt."*

As always, the moment that he made any connection between the Carnival and the memory of Melissa's kindness, Jonathan was snapped back into the nightmare-scape. Here, the Voice was in control, and Jonathan was helpless to obey.

He was pulled around the last corner of the path, and as the gnarled trunk of the final tree fell out of his vision, the entire Carnival spread out before him, rippling and undulating like the water of a stormy ocean. Unlike the real world, color oozed and dripped from every surface, assaulting him from every angle. It was the twisted joint vision of Nikola Tesla and Salvador Dali. The rivers of fluorescent hues slithered and swirled around the simple monstrosity that was the centerpiece of this cataclysmic collision of colors:

The Glass Globe.

The Glass Globe was, at its core, nothing more than a psychological prison, created by him and for him. He knew that it was not real in the tangible sense, but, even though its origin was psychological, it did not lessen the effect in any way.

In his mind, the Glass Globe looked like a horrific rendition of a child's snow globe, one that was large enough to trap a man—this man. It was devoid of any liquid, artificial snowflakes, or Rockwellian scene.

Jonathan had been imprisoned here over and over again for as long as he could remember, and for a variety of reasons: when The Voice decided that he was in trouble, when Jonathan found the sensory input of the everyday world overwhelming, or when he simply felt so scared he would have no choice but to escape to his prison. And then there were the times Jonathan would find himself captured within the Globe without a single memory of how or why he got there.

He never understood the logic behind his subconscious decision to hide from fear in a manifestation of his fears themselves.

At times, he wished that the Globe could be made of wood, or marble, or any other substance which was impenetrable by light. While the landscape around him seemed wrought from neon supernovas, it was what hung in the space above that scared him the most.

The space above the Carnival, while not the psychedelic collage that surrounded the Globe, was equally, if not more, twisted. Instead of stars or pure blackness, he was forced to watch a projection of the real world in real-time, reducing him to a mere spectator to his own words and actions. Once, he watched his arms as they reached for Melissa's slender neck, the necklace he had bought her as an anniversary gift shifting from left to right as she backed away from him half-heartedly, knowing she was cornered. Today, he witnessed glass shattering and spilling across the kitchen tile like stardust, herbs and spices crunching underfoot as he moved. He saw the microwave oven, its door wrenched from its hinges and slung through the window above the sink.

As he stood in the Glass Globe, Jonathan saw himself get up from the couch, and pull the broom from its place by the door. He begins to half-heartedly sweep the broken glass and wasted food into a pile in the center of the room, where he already knew that it would sit for at least a week or two before he would finally throw it away. Years ago he figured out that if he could keep actual physical reminders of his actions, he was less likely to behave in the same manner again, at least in the short term.

He would feel better, he always did. Every time he descended, he would eventually return to something which resembled what other people called "normal." The cycle would never end—up and down and up and down and up and down.

Rather than the episodes themselves, the transitions between the phases were what exhausted him the most. He already felt the inevitable weariness which would always follow a trip inside his own mind. Usually within half an hour, he would drop into a two-day slumber that resembled death itself, rising only to use the bathroom, then crawling back into bed.

It was during those times that Melissa would normally pick up around the house, do laundry, and get caught up on her reading.

Jonathan chuckled ruefully as he thought of how patient Melissa had been with him during the repetitive downward cycles, sometimes going so far as to provoke an argument in order to accelerate his inevitable descent—and eventual recovery—the psychological equivalent of yanking an adhesive bandage from the skin versus slowly pulling it away. The tiny sound of his laughter echoed off the spherical interior of the Glass Globe. For a fleeting moment, he could have sworn that the brilliant landscape dimmed ever so slightly, almost enough to where he could discern the path that led out of this hellhole.

In the real world, Jonathan let the broom fall to the linoleum floor with a loud clack, and shuffled back into the living room. He lay down on the old, broken sofa, the boards groaning as he stretched out his entire body on the cushions that were torn and bleeding their foam rubber interiors. His eyes were open, but he was still in the Globe, held there by the thought of the Voice.

"I told you that no one else cares about what happens to you; only I can understand, only I can sympathize."

The voice that sibilantly slithered into his mind was thin and reedy. Around the edges of the Globe a mist began to gather – not obscuring his vision, but rather taunting it, teasing it, never staying in one place for very long before darting somewhere else.

"Why do you fight me?"

"I don't like what you do," Jonathan answered, his voice weak, rough, and unused.

"You know that I keep you safe." The mist was growing in intensity, and starting to coalesce into a single form.

This was new.

The click of a key in a lock caused Jonathan to look away from the form of the Voice, which was now taking on a more humanoid appearance.

The door swung open, and the unthinkable happened.

Melissa walked into the living room, her large, green eyes drawn immediately to his supine form, and he could see that she had been crying. Her lips twisted up in a sad smile, one of resignation and defeat. She laid a key on the arm of the sofa, and reached behind her neck and unclasped the necklace that he had given her. She held the pendant in her palm, and let the chain fall into a puddle of gold-plated nickel threads around the tiny stone.

Fear slammed into him, and instantly the mist that was shaping the Voice took its final form.

Jonathan found himself staring into his own face.

"No, Melissa!" he called, frantically. He pounded his fists against the Glass Globe. It was to no avail, she would not hear him; she never heard him when the Voice forced him to hide in his "safe place." At least the Voice knew to let Melissa gather her things in peace and walk out of Jonathan's life, the same way Susan did, the same way Maria did, the same way Caroline did, the same way...

Again, Jonathan could hear laughter, but this time, it was not his chuckle that echoed inside the Glass Globe. This laugh belonged to the Voice.

"You never learn, do you?"

Jonathan remained silent. His alternate form began to circle the Globe, and for the first time, Jonathan felt as if he were an animal on display, nothing more than a creature trapped in a zoo.

Did he belong in a cage?

"Shut. Up." The Voice paused in his circuit, shocked by Jonathan's command. "What if I don't want to be safe?"

It was a question he had asked several times before. And it was always answered the same way:

"If I don't keep you safe, you will die" was the standard answer, and, by rote, it was given to him again.

But this time was... different. The Voice's words struck Jonathan in the chest like a cannonball, and true to the metaphor, Jonathan crumpled to the bottom of the Globe.

"I will always love you, Jonathan. Never forget that. And I will be there for you when you need me the most," Melissa was saying, tears streaming down her face.

Inside the Globe, Jonathan's eyes flew open when he heard Melissa's gentle, caring voice. Her eyes shifted between the necklace, still in the palm of her hand, to the key gleaming from the arm of the sofa. She inhaled slowly and deeply, held her breath for the briefest of moments, and then released it in a short, single, forceful blast.

"Call me when you're through the phase. I meant it when I said I would never abandon you." Resolved, she curled her fingers around the necklace, securing it in her hand, and picked up the key. Just as quietly as she had arrived, she walked out the door, locking it behind her. And by taking the key with her, Jonathan knew it meant one thing:

She could come back.

The next sound he heard was the mocking, taunting laughter of the Voice.

"I told you that she wouldn't last. No one can truly love a broken, twisted thing like you."

Jonathan still lay at the bottom of the Glass Globe, but he was not asleep. In fact, he felt stronger than he ever had when he was imprisoned in the sphere.

Melissa had taken the key. There had been no one before her—either friend or lover—who had returned once pushed to this stage, once witnessing the lowest of Jonathan's lows. He could feel Melissa's confidence in him move through his body, and as soon as he acknowledged this fact, he realized without delay that had been such a fool.

"What are you going to do now? You should really just stay in there forever. You'll be safer, you'll be protected. I can handle the world for you, you know."

Jonathan was confused. The Voice did not seem to comprehend that which Jonathan had already figured out. The Voice did not... could not know that Melissa's love for Jonathan could bring him strength.

"You're right," said Jonathan, "I can't handle the whole world." It was not a question. "But I can handle the mess that I made."

"What are you talking about?" asked the Voice, its form beginning to flicker, to snap in and out of focus. *"I mean, we'll need to get someone else to do the cleaning, and you are so good at attracting them. It's just too bad you can't keep them around for very long."*

"I don't need to keep anyone."

"You mean you can't keep anyone."

The Voice was increasing in volume, but now it sounded forced, strained. Jonathan looked up, and the Voice, his alter-ego, looked like a television channel that would not resolve fully into a proper picture, flickering in and out of existence with increasing rapidity.

"What you need to do is to keep just one person at a time. And when you drive them off, as you always do, there are plenty more to take their place."

"I only need to keep myself."

Jonathan stood up, his energy and strength surging as it never had before. And unlike every other time he escaped from his mental prison, he was not using his own energy. He was taking it from the Voice, from the landscape, and from the very fear that dragged him to this place every time the world became too much for him to handle.

At last, he understood: The Voice was not a separate person; it was just one part of many that made up the man that was Jonathan.

The days of the Voice calling the shots were over.

Jonathan raised his fist and was shocked to discover a hammer clenched there. Not the type of hammer one would use to hang a picture, but a hammer similar to one that a Norse god would wield in battle.

Jonathan smiled as one of his favorite mottoes sprang into his mind: "Go big or go home." He raised the hammer to strike.

"I do not keep other people," Jonathan yelled, the echo of his voice off the Glass Globe almost as deafening as dull thuds that sounded every time the hammer made contact. Over and over he struck the Globe, forcing more energy into each subsequent blow. "That is what you do. You keep me here when you want to, when you think I need it."

"What are you doing?" asked the Voice, desperate now. *"You don't have the strength for this."*

"You're right, I don't," said Jonathan, simply. "But *you* do."

Jonathan barely had time to register the surprise in the eyes of the form of the Voice before it dissolved into complete nothingness as the hammer struck the fatal blow to the Glass Globe. It shattered into a million pieces, all of which blew away on an wind which he could neither see, nor hear, nor feel, fading quickly into oblivion. Gone was the nightmare landscape; the path through the woods—lit from an unseen source—gentle, inviting, and welcome.

Jonathan wasted no time running full sprint back up the path that led out of his mind, his prison, never noticing that the path, and the trees on either side of it, disappeared as he passed them, not needed anymore.

A few hours later, after Jonathan had bagged the last of the trash from the destroyed kitchen, and carried the bags and the ruined microwave out to the dumpster. He took the few items that Melissa had left behind, wrapped them carefully in clean, dry newspaper, and placed them gently in a cardboard box, using more of the newspaper to fill the gaps between her possessions. He placed the box on the top shelf of the coat closet, and resolved to decide what to do with it later.

He, of course, would want Melissa to stay, but she needed to stay out of desire, not requirement. He hoped that she would discuss with him that which brought them to this point before making any decisions, and felt confident that she would. She had always been more pragmatic than he, the logical yin to his creative yang.

Go big or go home, he thought.

He took a deep breath and pushed back the curtains. As Jonathan looked outside, he expected to see the same inky blackness that usually colored his vision. For as long as he could remember, the world existed in hues of gray and beige, but now everything had changed.

He saw the sky purpling in anticipation of dawn, the barest hint of orange at the seam of the horizon. Jonathan released the breath he had been unconsciously holding. He did not know why this sight made him happy, but an inability to understand the cause should never prevent a person from enjoying its effect.

It was morning.

Jonathan guessed it was time for coffee. He might even use that aromatic Turkish blend Melissa had discovered at the farmer's market down the street. It was a blend that they both loved, and although the aroma of the brew may not bring Melissa to his door, it would at least bring the thought of her to the sanctuary of his mind.

And that, for now, would be good enough.

BIG RED
AND THE
WETSAWANNAKAH
COUNTY P. T. A.

FRANK IRVINE HATES the first week of December.

As an educator, he finds the no-man's land between Thanksgiving and Christmas rife with more distractions than he feels are remotely necessary, even given the holiday season. There seems to be candy everywhere, which makes the students in his morning classes hyperactive, yet renders those after lunch nearly comatose. He briefly thinks they should make coffee as freely available to the students as they do the faculty, but quickly dismisses that from his mind when he realizes the sheer volume of bathroom break requests he would be forced to deny.

Aside from student behavior, there are plenty of other reasons to despise these scant few weeks before the winter break begins. Some of the more frivolous teachers insist on decorating the doors of their classrooms to celebrate the season, though Frank sees this as merely evidence of why these individuals are teaching subjects other than art. Cameron Preparatory Academy does enforce a somewhat strict dress code, but it is during this time of year that students choose to accessorize their barrettes, earrings, book bags, and blazers with all manner of holiday-themed ornaments, including every shape and size of sleigh bells. While not strictly forbidden by the dress code, Frank feels that there should be at least limits based on social propriety.

"Miss Martin?" he calls out across the quad. The blonde cheerleading captain does not even look up, but continues to hold court by a fountain that has not worked since the Eisenhower administration.

"Miss Martin!"

Kathleen Martin's head snaps up quickly, locking eyes with him.

"Yes, Mister Irvine?" she asked innocently. "Is something wrong?"

"Yes, come here. I need to discuss your... your... your bells."

At the word "bells," Kathleen's courtiers explode into a giggling mass, gathering books and bags, and heading toward their next class. Kathleen slips her messenger bag over her shoulder, and sashays over to where Frank stands, the toe of his black loafer tapping impatiently.

"Mister Irvine, don't you like my... bells?" she asks, playing at being coy. "Everyone so far today has loved my bells."

Immediately, Frank's eyes drop to the accessories in question, each dangling from a neatly tied red ribbon, meant to form a rudimentary brooch. However, instead of wearing the pins on a lapel, or even just below the shoulder, Kathleen had chosen to place them on the very front of her bust, right where her nipples would have been, had they not been clothed in the standard-issue navy blue sweater vest.

As Frank, a teacher, stares at Kathleen Martin's legendary bosom—it has been rumored that one could park a '67 Buick in its shadow—Kathleen shakes her shoulders, the motion traveling down her body, causing her breasts to sway and the bells to softly ring.

Now she is just screwing with him.

Frank realizes that he has been maneuvered into staring fully at the head cheerleader's chest, and now she is overtly taunting him.

"Take them off. Now. Get to class. Now."

Kathleen tosses her head back and laughs, turning to head down one of the many corridors that made up the humanities building.

"Sure, Mister Irvine," she calls over her shoulder. "Whatever you say."

As she disappears around a corner, Frank realizes two things. First, he should have given the offer from St. Ignatius' Academy for Boys further consideration, and second, and more importantly, he has left his coffee back in the teacher's lounge.

"Dammit," sighs Frank, to the empty quadrangle.

The teacher's lounge at Cameron is supposed to provide a place of respite from the onslaught of stress that comes alongside the opportunity to mold the young minds unfortunately contained in the bodies of hormonal teenagers. It is meant to be a place of solace, a place of quiet.

However, when Frank walks back through the door of the large room dotted with sofas and easy chairs, it is none of these things. The same wretched soul responsible for the gaudy display on the door of the room next to Frank's seems to have allowed her decorating skills to metastasize into here as well. Silver tinsel is draped everywhere, reflecting the already too bright light and not helping Frank's headache one bit.

Joann Taylor, one of the French teachers, is sitting in the center of the room, her obesity wedged into a single, high-sided chair which should have caused Dr. Wright, the physics teacher sitting across from her, to question the structural integrity of the furniture.

Frank huffs and begins to weave his way over to where he can see his coffee cup, no longer steaming but still quite full, on a table on the far side of the room. He hopes to simply slip in and slip out, unnoticed by his colleagues, but those hopes, like all his hopes during this time of year, are soon nothing but a memory.

"Fraaaaaaaaaaank!" squeals Joann, giving Frank's monosyllabic name three full seconds of duration. This is but one of Frank's many issues with the French teacher. "Come join us!"

"No, thank you," replies Frank politely, returning to his quest. "I've got to get back to my classroom and get ready for next period."

"Oh, pish," responds Joann, waving his excuse off with her fat, stubby hand. "You've got almost an hour before you have to be back. I saw you talking to Kathleen Martin in the quad."

Frank freezes, and his face burns with shame as he instantly and completely recalls the exchange, including the overstated ogling of the cheerleader's bosom. Turning around, Frank sees Joann's meaty slab of a hand patting the armrest of the chair next to hers.

He knows he is trapped. If he blows her off, she will still gossip, and if he stays, he has a chance, albeit slight, of ensuring that the truth is at least presented.

He chooses to share the sofa with Dr. Wright, however, rather than risk being struck in the head by chair-shrapnel should the mass of Joann Taylor finally overtake the engineering of the furniture.

"There's a girl like that in every school," begins Frank, suddenly realizing that in addition to Joann and Dr. Wright, he has been joined by Miss Holmes, who teaches Spanish, and the Missuses Adams, Charles and Lincoln, who all three teach English. Rounding out their little group is Coach Hook, who unlike his literary nautical namesake, is in possession of both of his hands. "They think that the rules don't apply to them, and that they're God's gift to the school."

"It is a bit difficult for her to be… unobtrusive," observes one of the English teachers, but Frank cannot tell which one. Honestly, the way they go everywhere with each other reminded him, more than once, of the three witches from *Macbeth*.

"I'm surprised she doesn't have to wear a back brace," Hook interjects.

"How lovely," responded another of the Witches Three. "Leave it to you to judge based on appearance."

"I'm not judging," retorts Hook. "Those things are biological facts. And did you see where she put those bells?"

"Frank did," says Joann, a wicked grin barely concealed on her face. "From what I saw, he got a very good look."

Frank has to get control of the story again, and suddenly, he realizes just how he will do it.

"Like I said, there's one in every class. One person who is my cross to bear the entire year, and who will, at least at one point, make sure that my life is a living hell," he says, happy to hear the chatter cease around him. "I still remember my first year teaching, when I met the girl who would become my nemesis by the end of the year."

"Who was she?" asks a voice from somewhere off to the left, but Frank is already descending into his memory.

"I can't remember her name," he says, "her real name, at least. But everyone from the principal of the school on down called her Big Red."

Wetsawannakah County, Alabama, is located somewhere between Montgomery and Birmingham, and cannot be reached directly by way of interstate. It held only three schools, aptly named "Elementary," "Middle," and "High," for there was no need of distinction when there was only one of each. While the other buildings in the area may have changed over the years, the schools had, surprisingly, stayed the same, with the same administrators and teachers, clinging to their careers until the school board either reduced them to an "aide" or euthanized them outright.

Frank stares into the shocked eyes of his colleagues, and suddenly realizes his mistake.

"They retired them," he says, shocked that he had to make such a clarification. "Did you really think they had them dragged out and shot?"

"Well," says Coach Hook, "it is Alabama. Coulda been why they're called the *crimson* tide? Right? Right?" Coach Hook looks around the room and sees that no one is interested in his play on words. "But if it was in the middle of nowhere, why the hell did you want to go there?"

"My dear coach," Frank replies, "I did not choose to go there. I went because I did not have a choice."

Despite his snobbery in his later years, Frank did not start his career a crotchety old man. He sprang forth from the graduating class of Florida State University's School of Education dead in the middle of the class, but with high enough marks to at least earn his certificate and allow him to teach. He did his student teaching at a small, out of the way charter school just outside Tallahassee, and when it came time to look for jobs in the Florida school system, he was shocked when he discovered that there were exactly zero.

Expanding his search, he was even more shocked to discover that while, yes, a private institution would come with higher pay, they also required more experience, one commodity that Frank did not have. In the end, the Wetsawannakah County school board had made the last-minute decision to let Mrs. Franklin, who had taught English at the high school since Shakespeare was working on his first manuscript, "spend more time with her family."

Frank got her old job—Freshman English and Senior English, which consisted of mostly composition instruction, a small amount of reading for the ninth graders, and a near-global tour of literature for those about to graduate and go out into the world. The senior curriculum had been broken into smaller modules, each focusing on a specific subset of literature. Frank was amazed at the variety offered to the students at such a small, rural school, and soon, was heading north and west, until he reached Birmingham. He then had to double-back, and then doubled-back again, because, honestly, he managed to miss the exit twice in a row.

"Was it really that small?" asks Joann, incredulity in her voice.

"Yes. Only four or five roads—all of them county roads, mind you—led in or out of the so-called town. Really, it was just a gathering of buildings at a crossroads more than anything else. The county itself is huge, but honestly, in that part of the country, I personally think that the population has an inverse relationship to the length of the county name."

"An inverse... what?" asks Joann. Frank is pleased that she is flustered. Frank loves it when Joann is flustered.

"It means that the longer the name, the less people live there," barks the coach, clearly wanting to hear more. Frank does not disappoint.

His classroom was sparse, but he had only arrived the weekend before, so he had resolved spend the coming weekend fixing it up. He had already found an apartment, furnished it, and had picked out posters of famous authors for the walls of his classroom, but would have to wait until Saturday to travel to the Wal-Mart in the nearby metropolis of Wetumpka in order to get frames for them.

After spending the entire morning schooling freshmen in the art of writing correctly, he was relieved when his first senior class filed into the room after lunch. Every single student had known each other practically since they were in utero, but the quick glances in his direction as they comfortably chatted and socialized with each other did not go unnoticed.

He was the new guy, after all.

Only one person in the entire class was not engaged with her peers, but instead, had a Cover Girl compact open, gazing so intently into it that Frank thought for a moment it may, in fact contain the answer to life's ultimate questions. Frank suddenly dismissed the thought when he saw what the young woman did next.

Without breaking her gaze, she reached a hand toward the front of her hair, which had been teased into an ovoid pouf, its color somewhere between "fire engine" and "blood bank." The more Frank looked at her hair, the more he realized it was the color of what happened when a fire engine crashed into a blood bank.

Slowly, deliberately, she grasped a single lock of hair from the pouf, and shifted it a half-inch to her left. Double-checking her work in the mirror, she nodded once to herself, and snapped the compact shut with such force Frank was sure she had shattered the glass. She then turned to gaze at him.

The young woman known by everyone as "Big Red" sat and stared, her mouth a straight line across a face that was perfectly round. Her base makeup looked like it had been applied with a spray gun, and her blue eyeshadow slathered on with a garden trowel. Her face was a collision of color, and just like a train wreck, Frank found he could not look away.

Thankfully, the bell rang, snapping him from his reverie. After introducing himself, Frank announced that they would be starting with Southern literature—Faulkner to be precise.

In reviewing the previous years' syllabi, Frank noticed that there had been very few changes from year to year. Of course, the hallmarks of literature were there, but it seemed that only the hallmarks had made the course. He approached the principal about adding a couple of new works, and was told that yes, he could add the works, but was also reminded that people "in these parts" tended "not to like change." Frank decided to start with only a short story.

William Faulkner's "A Rose for Emily," despite the long and, in Frank's mind, somewhat tedious exposition, ends with a twist that leaves the reader as breathless as if they had just watched a film by Alfred Hitchcock. Subtle in its delivery, that single strand of surprise shocks nearly every reader the first time through, reduced only to anticipated horror with each subsequent re-reading. A short piece, he assigned it on a Thursday, to be discussed the very next day.

"We gotta read the whole thing t'night?" asked Big Red from the back of the room.

"Relax," Frank reassured her. "It's not that long. It will take you half an hour tops."

"Oh, okay. It'll at least give me something to do while I'm getting my hair did."

"Done," corrected Frank, out of reflex more than anything else. "You get your hair done. Someone did your hair."

"Whatever," said Big Red, and turned back to the book she was reading. Frank had noticed twenty minutes earlier that while every other student had the assigned book in front of them, the book held in Big Red's had a cover depicting what can only be described as the world's most handsome pirate, complete with a frocked wench arching her back in a style he had only seen at the ballet.

He never realized wenches could be so flexible.

The bell rang and the students filed out before he could admonish her further.

The next day, the students were practically buzzing when they sat down, and Frank felt a swelling of pride. They were chomping at the proverbial bit to discuss the story, and Frank eagerly dove into the topic with a passion that is generally only found in those who have recently graduated from college, and have yet to become jaded by the system.

Frank had no idea this would be one of the last times he would ever feel that joy. He was so happy that he barely noticed Big Red fixing her make-up for the entire fifty-minute period.

Back in the present, the Witches Three are eagerly dissecting Faulkner's story as if they were before a white-board and the faculty in the lounge were their class. A few more teachers—two math and another science—have joined their little group, and when Frank speaks, everyone hangs on his every word. Deep inside his soul, Frank feels a stirring similar to the day that he first discussed "A Rose for Emily" with that class, though now that feeling is hard to pinpoint, buried under cynicism and apathy.

Frank clears his throat, and even the trio of English teachers falls silent.

Things continued in the same fashion for the rest of the year. After Southern Literature came Victorian Literature, and after that, a relatively recent addition—African-American Literature. The final module of the year was Coming of Age Literature, a category which Frank had been looking forward to for one hundred and forty of the one hundred and eighty days of the school calendar.

There were the usual suspects—John Knowles' A Separate Peace, *particularly, but Frank chose this module to make his most drastic changes to the curriculum. Again he approached the principal, who gave his rubber-stamp approval and his standard warning.*

Frank wanted to show movies in class.

Not movies of the books that they were reading, but movies instead of some of the books they were reading. The film industry had come a long way, and while decent adaptations of some novels did exist, they were few and far between. However, there were some gems of the cinema, and while he would never dream of showing something as racy as The Graduate, *he thought such fare as* My Dog Skip *would be well tolerated. He even tacked on John Hughes'* The Breakfast Club *for good measure, feeling that the ensemble cast would resonate with his own class.*

In addition to the films, he also chose to add a book that he thought should have been there from the beginning. How the school had managed to have a class called Coming of Age Literature and not require the reading of J. D. Salinger's The Catcher in the Rye *completely escaped Frank. He quickly and quietly corrected that oversight, and chose to have the students write a paper (worth one-half their grade for the class) comparing themselves to Holden Caufield.*

The due date for the paper arrived, and he walked up and down the aisles between the desks, thanking each student by name as he took their papers. Over the course of the year, he had made it a point to learn the name of each and every student in all of his classes, and became friendly with most of them.

As he reached the desk in front of the one in which Big Red sat, he saw that there was no paper on her desk. He almost faltered while speaking to Julie Bender, but recovered quickly. Two steps later, he was once again facing Big Red's round face, but this time, a self-satisfied grin taunted him.

"Where is your assignment?" asked Frank, honestly wanting to hear neither her usual flimsy excuse, nor the mangled English with which it would be spoken.

"Didn't do it," she answered, daring him to ask for an explanation. Frank, unfortunately, did precisely that.

"Why not?"

"My momma said I didn't have to read that book," said Big Red, her smile growing to full, crooked brilliance.

"Very well," said Frank, and moved over to the next aisle.

It was a calculated risk. On one hand, Frank knew that he had a lot to cover and very little time in which to do it. On the other, he knew that Big Red, if anything, was a diva. She loved being center-stage, and simply denying her an audience should cow her into silence.

Needless to say, Frank miscalculated.

"Dontcha wanna know why?" bellowed Big Red, rising from her seat.

"Not really," said Frank without a trace of concern. "Do sit down, though."

He collected another paper and thanked another student when he was assaulted by Big Red's thunderous voice yet again.

"My momma wants to know why you would even assign that book," she shouted, still standing by her desk.

Frank turned what he was sure was a truly apathetic gaze on the unruly student, but was shocked when he saw the look in Big Red's eyes: fear.

For the first time in her entire seventeen years of life, Big Red was not sure of the argument she was making. They had been discussing the book for the past week, and while a few students found its tone a bit on the depressing side, most of them regularly engaged with Frank in a near-lively debate.

It reassured Frank that he had chosen wisely the path of the educator, and the renewed interest in his class had already brought the skeptical-but-approving principal to his door twice with talk of an extended contract.

In the split-second he had to reflect, Frank suddenly realized why Big Red seemed apprehensive. The more the students engaged with him, the more they disengaged from her.

She was alone, and as Frank could obviously see, being alone made Big Red scared.

"I assigned, ahem" Frank had to clear his throat to buy a few seconds. "I assigned the book because it's a quintessential representation of coming-of-age literature in America. I can guarantee you that nearly all other high schools teach it, some in the lower grades. I assigned it because it is a masterpiece, and I thought you would get something out of it, even if you hated it."

"Well, how could I learn something if I hated it?" asked Big Red, clearly grasping at straws.

"I guess we'll never know," said Frank, finally settling behind his desk and getting ready to move on to the next topic.

"I guess we will," said Big Red, sitting down as well. "You can explain it to my momma yourself. She's gonna be here tomorrow night for the meetin'."

Frank had completely forgotten about the PTA meeting.

"I'm so glad we don't have the PTA here," says Joann, herself a veteran of the public school system. "Parents pay way too much to have us raise their children. They obviously don't want to be involved in their kids' education."

"Careful, darling" purrs Frank, and then quickly corrects his misstep, changing his tone back to one of aggravation. "Someone might think you actually care."

"I do care," retorts Joann sharply. "Writing a check, no matter how big, can never be an expression of love."

"Do you mind if I continue?" asks Frank.

"If you must," is her response.

There are days he really hates this woman.

The Wetsawannakah County P.T.A. held its meetings in the school gymnasium, the acoustics of which effectively neutralized the voice of any speaker. Frank endured the occasional meetings with something a little more than boredom, but a lot less than excitement. There was one portion of the agenda, however, that he dreaded above all:

Parent Concerns.

Parent Concerns was essentially open-mike night for any parent who wished to question the motives or actions of any of the faculty members. Early in his career, the principal had been caught off guard when several teachers, ironically not present at the meeting, had been accused of shirking their duties in the classroom as well. From that point on, attendance on the dais was mandatory, in the event that a teacher should come under fire. With the grace of a state governor caught unaware by an ice storm predicted a week prior, he ensured that there were plenty of targets at the next press conference.

Tonight, however, something hung in the air. The rest of the meeting went by in a blur, and before Frank knew it, they were at the dreaded point in the agenda. Frank had seen Big Red hanging in the back of the room, and had been desperately searching for her mother, Priscilla, or "Prissy" as people tended to call her.

Frank did not honestly know if this was an adjective or a nickname.

The principal asked if anyone had anything they wished to say, and the gym went as silent as a grave. From the back, a slight woman, nowhere near Big Red's stature, started forward, and Frank breathed a sigh of relief.

His breath caught in his through as she drew closer, and saw the same unmistakable round face on Prissy as he did every day when he looked at the last chair on the last row in the first class after lunch.

Big Red had a mother, and she had arrived. Before she had even reached the podium and microphone, her hand flew up, finger pointed directly at Frank, and she yelled loudly enough for everyone to hear.

"I wanna talk about that man."

The end of her sentence coincided with her arrival at the podium, causing feedback to blare from the speakers and all in attendance to wince. She backed away from the microphone, and restated her demand.

"I wanna talk about that man. The one who asked my little girl to read that book."

"Yes," said the principal. "Frank, could you join me up here, please?"

Coward, thought Frank as he stepped up next to the principal. Prissy continued.

"I wanna know where you get the nerve to change what we been learnin' 'round these parts?" she asked, but did not wait for an answer. "I went to this school. I took English at this school. And there ain't a damn thing wrong with me."

And still, Prissy continued.

"You dare, sir," she said as she leaned forward, "you dare to ask my daughter to read that piece of filth. Then you have the gall to ask her to write a paper on it? Just where do you get off doin' that, huh?"

The pregnant pause apparently indicated that Prissy was, in fact, waiting for a response, but Frank was at a loss. The Catcher in the Rye may have been a bit edgy, and yes, some educators had even been fired in the past for assigning it. But that was in the early 1960's; since those days it had become an allegory for angst and teenage rebellion.

"I don't understand," he began, keeping his voice low. "I know the book may have some more mature language, but I can assure you, there's nothing in the book that most, if not all of the students in the class haven't heard before."

"Vulgar language?" shrieked Prissy, her voice jumping an octave, her tone resembling the amplifier's feedback from a moment ago. "There's vulgar language in it too? I just had to read the title to know it was pure-tee-filth. I mean, honestly!"

Frank was stunned. He had no idea what this woman was talking about.

"I'm sorry, Mrs. ..." began Frank, only to be stopped by Prissy once more.

"Vulgar? You asked my darling little girl to read something called Catch Her In The Raw." She pounded her fist on the podium with every word of the misspoken title, as if she could physically drive her point home. "Where do you get off doin' that?"

Suddenly, Prissy's support was gone, and there was absolutely no sound in the gym. After a few seconds of total silence, the audience exploded into laughter, the peals echoing off wooden stands, hard floors, and a vaulted ceiling, its volume deafening, its momentum crushing. Frank was using every ounce of restraint to hold back his own laughter, and after quick glance to his right, saw that the principal was doing the same.

Prissy, the mother of Big Red, was standing center stage, casting about frantically until she realized that everyone was laughing at her.

Unlike the gymnasium in Frank's story, there is pure silence in the faculty lounge of Cameron Preparatory Academy.

"What?" asks Coach Hook. "I mean...even I know the title, and I'm a dumb jock."

"I don't know if Big Red mispronounced it when she was at home and Prissy took off and didn't look back, or if Prissy was, in fact, illiterate. I didn't stay long enough to find out. I moved away that summer, and have been up here ever since."

"What happened to Big Red?" prompts Joann, her eyes flicking to the clock on the wall as a silent reminder that they are about to run out of time.

"She was in the back of the gym, and as soon as her mother said... what she said, she bolted. Teenagers will be teenagers, I guess. The kids talked about it for a few days, then they forgot about it. There was only a couple of weeks left in the year, anyway. Soon enough, they all graduated, Big Red included."

"Did you ever see her again?" asks one of the English teachers, the three rising as one. Frank seriously considered buying them matching black outfits and pointed hats as a joke, then remembered that he was not supposed to have a sense of humor at work.

"Once. She came into my classroom room right after graduation but before school ended. She wanted to thank me."

"Thank you?" asks the coach. "What for? Making her a laughingstock?"

"Shockingly, no," says Frank, moving back to his long-forgotten coffee, so he could dump it out and refill it before his next class. The climax of the story is over, and his audience is starting to dwindle.

"She told me that up until that night in the gym, she thought her mother was absolutely right about everything. She wanted to thank me for attempting to open her eyes, and was sorry it took such a public spectacle to do so. She said that she would continue to take her mother's advice, but it was time she started making her own decisions."

"Oddly insightful for someone who did her make-up all year," says Joann, hefting her weight out of the chair and walking toward the door just as the last member of Frank's audience, Coach Hook, walks out of the room.

"She had her moments, that's for sure," says Frank.

The room is now empty except for Frank and Joann, the latter pausing at the door, turning to face Frank.

"You know that I know," says Joann, "that what really happened was you were only called into the principal's office with Big Red and her mother, and there wasn't the whole P.T.A. production. I swear that story gets more and more grandiose every time you tell it."

"I know," counters Frank, before placing a quick kiss on his wife's cheek. Joann uses her maiden name at work; it makes for less hassle, though it is the worst-kept secret at the school. "But that's why I teach English, and you don't."

"The only reason you teach English, my dear, is because the school has yet to make Twenty-First Century Bullshit an actual course," she says, once again turning to go.

"However, if you pick up milk on you way home, I promise to never mention Kathleen Martin's bells again."

"Of course, dear," smirks Frank, and turns his attention back to his coffee.

MY LIFE AS A FAIRY TALE

APUNZEL

I AM ELEVEN YEARS OLD, and I am locked in a Tower.

Mind you, this is not a tower in the literal sense. I am not hundreds of feet off the ground in a circular building of stone construction, and although I do not know what a "rampart" is at my age, I cannot see one from where I sit.

Instead, I am in the closet between two classrooms on the third floor of the building that houses the students who have not yet attained the seventh grade. My cheeks are still wet from tears that have spilled unrestrained down the blotchy skin of my face that is, in addition to my head, too large for my body.

Looking back, this is not the only time that I have been sequestered as a result of my education, or better, my inability to fully integrate with my education.

The first time I can remember being set apart was at Sweet Stream Elementary School in the fourth grade. In my four-year career at this public institution of learning (I skipped the first grade), I studied under, with one exception, wonderful teachers. Unlike my peers, I enjoyed going to school; the work was laughably easy, and I often found myself with my assignment completed and time still on the clock. I had shown up to kindergarten already knowing how to work multiplication tables and read books on my own; the latter skill my ironically-named teacher, an African-American whom we called "Miss White," put to use in the classroom, placing me center stage to read aloud to the class. By the third grade I had been moved into the "gifted program." The school board provided a break to the tedium of spelling quizzes and art projects by busing us to an unused high school nearby. Although our tiny steps echoed loudly through the empty corridors, we nonetheless learned how to properly cook and eat Indian food, we discussed the technical aspects of *The Empire Strikes Back*, and studied not only how to play chess, but how to win the game. While I am quite sure there was some overreaching educational aspect to the whole curriculum, to me the best part was getting to leave school on a semi-regular basis.

My teachers back at Sweet Stream were not only under-standing, but they even helped me helped me catch up on my work. All in all, everything was fine.

On the first day of the fourth grade, I met the woman who would be the first to divert my life onto a path that was completely new and totally unexpected. As everyone knows, when you are eight years old, your teachers do not have first names. My teacher's last name was "Snave" and her first name was, of course "Missus." My mother seemed to think that Missus Snave's first name was really "That Bitch," but I found out later that it was Laura.

Missus Snave was quite the enforcer and would tolerate no disruption to her routine. Knowledge was written in white chalk on a green chalkboard. Children kept their mouths closed and their ears open, and students were never encouraged to speak. Her reason was always the same and always offered without prompting: "God gave us two ears and one mouth, which means listening is twice as important as talking."

Aside from the gifted program's field trips, my only respite from Missus Snave was that I got to walk three doors down the hall to Mr. Flynn's classroom, where I took math with a different group of children, and more importantly, a different teacher. Mr. Flynn had a shiny forehead, and his hair looked exactly like my father's. It turned out that they both were merely wearing toupees, but the resemblance gave me enough comfort that I actually began to excel in math. Mr. Flynn encouraged us to participate, and while we were not allowed to run amok, he constantly asked us questions and actually expected us to answer.

It made it damn near impossible for me to swap *Star Wars* cards with my friend Gary, who sat next to me during the class.

For the most part, the year went by without much out of the ordinary. Halfway through the fourth grade, however, Missus Snave began to pin notes to my clothing to ensure that they reached my mother (a move I still feel was not only unnecessary but exceedingly embarrassing). They invariably would detail my most recent transgression, be it misbehavior, an inability to sit still, or my insistence there was "a rat" in "sep-a-rate," no matter how many times she wrote it as "seperate" on the blackboard. And while she neither pinned a scarlet letter "A" to my shirt nor hung an albatross around my neck, the paper seemed just as noticeable and just as heavy. While I would remove it from my clothes as soon as I was out from under her near-constant gaze, I still had to walk around with it flapping on my shirt for the majority of the day.

One day, I forgot to take it off. I did not realize my mistake until I was walking toward my mother's brown Pontiac LeMans station wagon. I was wondering why her eyes kept getting bigger and bigger, then a short burst of wind caused the paper to fly up into my face. I stopped dead in my tracks.

She got out of the car, walked over to where I stood, and took the note from my clothes. She read it over, and after instructing me to "sit in the car" and "not move," she stalked into the school building.

After what seemed like an eternity, the door to the school exploded outward. All the other kids had gone home, and only my mother's blocky station wagon remained parked in the drive outside the school. My mother strode toward the car, much more quickly than she had left it. After climbing into the driver's seat, she fumbled with the keys for quite a while before turning them in the ignition. I noticed her hands were shaking.

"That Bitch will never pin another damned thing to you ever again," she said, her tone low and her words even. And she was right; I not only never had a note pinned to me, That Bitch Laura never gave me another note to take home ever again.

Quite late in the year, almost to summer vacation, I found myself separated from my classmates completely. While the details of my actions are still cloudy in my memory, the "consequences of my actions," as the principal put them, are carved into my episodic memory with a great level of detail.

I was locked in a Tower.

The Tower, like the one that would follow it, was a closet. It was directly across the hall from the principal's office and had even dirtier floors than the rest of the school. Up until that point, the closet had been used to store a variety of items, including the prizes for the annual Halloween carnival, toilet paper, mops, brooms, and, more recently, a desk and a chair. Toward the back of the tiny room, there was an even tinier bathroom, packed to the ceiling with even more trappings of early childhood education and county-sponsored maintenance.

The desk and the chair seemed out of place, until I realized that the closet was now ready to store me.

The day I was placed in my Tower, I did not tell my parents. The next morning, when I was dropped off at school, I reported to Missus Snave's room as usual. But, as soon as the roll was called, I was escorted to the principal's office, given my assignments for the day, and shut into my Tower. I had it all done before eleven o'clock in the morning. After being escorted to the lunchroom, I returned with my tray, and ate in solitude. My tray was taken back for me, and the afternoon was spent exploring My Room. In addition to the toys from the Halloween carnival (several of which accidentally fell into my backpack), I found several books of all shapes and sizes, and I settled down to read.

To be honest, I personally had no issue with the arrangement; I had no close friends in my class, and other than Gary, my *Star Wars* trading card partner from Mr. Flynn's math class, I could not think of a single person who missed me.

I quickly settled into a routine: mornings were spent on schoolwork, afternoons were split between reading the books I found on the forgotten shelves in the closet, and appropriating more toys from the Halloween carnival supplies. After all, one could never have too many plastic skull necklaces and spider rings. I kept my mouth shut about the entire situation.

It was either day eight or ten and, for me, everything was going well. I had returned home, and my mother was making beef stew for dinner. I was sitting at the kitchen table pretending to do homework, while actually planning a strategy to avoid the stew. My father arrived home from work, his suit jacket over his shoulder, his tie loosened, and his top shirt button unbuttoned. He leaned down to kiss my mother on the cheek, stealing a glance into the huge iron pot which she was slowly stirring.

"Double, double, toil and trouble," he said, his eyes lighting up at the sight of the stew. It was one of his favorite meals, and was always served alongside hot, homemade cornbread from a black, cast iron skillet.

On hearing my father's words, I stopped my work and held my poorly sharpened pencil over the paper. I could not believe my ears; I had read those exact words earlier that day. I had found the book, well-worn and bearing a single sword-wielding figure on the cover, on the old, dilapidated bookshelf in my Tower, and was drawn to it immediately. First, it was a play; second, it started out with witches. My love of science fiction transitioned easily to fantasy.

"Fire burn and cauldron bubble." I was thrilled to be able to provide the next line.

My mother's hand froze over the stew, and both she and my father turned together to look at me.

"Where did you learn that, son?" he asked his voice light and casual.

"Read it at school," I responded, fear creeping into my heart. Had I done something wrong? I mentally ran though the layout of our house, trying to see if there was a closet here that could be turned into a Tower.

"You read that at school? Do you know what it's from?" my father asked.

"*Macbeth*." Satisfied that there were no potential Towers at home, I answered much more confidently. "It's by William Shakespeare. I read it today."

"You read the whole play-y-y?" my mother interjected, her voice rising slightly in the end. She seemed scared rather than happy. I hoped I had not messed up. Again. "When did you have time to read the whole play?"

"It's actually one of his shorter plays, if you consider..." my father began, but my mother was quick to close that discussion.

"Not the time, Richard!"

"Well, it is," he mumbled, looking conspiratorially at me. He seemed almost proud of what I had done.

"When did you read *Macbeth*?" my mother repeated her question, left hand placed firmly on her hip, the wooden stirring spoon turned backwards and dripping broth on the kitchen floor.

"I read it this afternoon while I was in My Room. It was there with another book, called *Hamlet*, although that one was bad. Everyone dies in the..." My words fall off; I remembered that I had not told my parents about my new educational arrangement.

"What do you mean 'Your Room'?"

My mother's question would lead to a very interesting dinner, one during which they never noticed that I had barely touched my beef stew, that I left my glass half-full of milk, and that my sister was, for once, blissfully silent. I told them about My Room, and what I did during the day. My father kept looking at my mother, finally reaching out and taking her hand. It was weird: during the meal she kept getting redder and shaking more, but her voice never got louder. Strangely, it seemed to grow calmer the further the meal progressed.

Before finishing her meal, my mother had gotten up and stormed back to their bedroom, and even in the kitchen we could hear her voice through the walls. My father let me go from dinner without finishing, which was odd, but I guessed that it was a special occasion.

As I got up from the table and headed down the hallway, my father called after me. "Hey son? I liked Macbeth better m'self, too." My father's admission, in his simple folksy drawl, began to calm my worried nerves.

Before I could completely relax, however, my mother's shout broke through the bedroom door: "Still not the point, Richard!"

My mother had a meeting with the principal and That Bitch Snave the very next morning in order to determine how best to handle me for the remainder of the school year. I waited outside the Principal's office, the gray-haired woman who was not-my-grandmother glancing at me from time to time, her smile soft, her eyes gentle. I could hear doors opening and closing, and soon I could hear my mother's voice echo down the cinder-block hallway.

"Open the door. I want to see where you put my son."

After my mother had been shown my Tower, it was decided that I would still be placed on my own, but would instead work with the Special Education teacher, Miss Mellibee. She had a classroom close to Missus Snave, but she hardly ever had anyone in there. Miss Mellibee was younger than most of the teachers at the school, and was very pretty, with long, straight brown hair and just the right amount of makeup.

If I thought that My Tower the best thing to happen since I had been consigned to a year with Missus Snave, I was wrong. Miss Mellibee would not only talk to me while I did my work, she would also answer my questions, and when she did have students in her room, I got to be her Helper. For the first time since I had started the fourth grade, I felt comfortable with my surroundings.

When the school year came to an end, I was sorry to have to go. On the very last day, I asked Miss Mellibee if she would be my teacher the next year, and if I would be her Helper.

She laughed her little laugh that she often laughed when I asked her a question, and said that she was "not sure." Having dealt with grown-ups for at least four or five years, I knew that "not sure" always meant "no." I cleaned out my desk and headed for the pick-up area so I could climb into my mother's Pontiac LeMans station wagon for what would be the last drive home from Sweet Stream Elementary School. I only made one stop; I walked into my old classroom so I could get That Bitch Snave to sign my yearbook.

I never knew what she truly desired to inscribe inside the cover, I was pretty sure "Good Luck!" was not it.

The next fall I started as a fifth-grader at the very prestigious and private Wormwood Academy, forty-five minutes away from our home. A year later, however, we moved closer to the school and now lived only a mile and a half away from the campus. I would remain at this school all the way through the twelfth grade; it simply seemed logical to shorten the commute.

I traded shorts and tank tops for slacks and golf shirts emblazoned with the name of the school where the left pocket should have been. When the weather got colder, the golf shirts went away, only to be replaced with button-down collars, ties, and navy blue blazers with the school's crest stitched to them.

The work here was more difficult, but I still excelled. In sixth grade I found out that we would be reading a translation of *The Odyssey*, one of my favorite stories. When I was five, my parents had given me a copy of d'Aulaire's *Book of Greek Myths*. It was my most-read book, and its large pages and colorful images kept me enraptured for hours. My father would sometimes pull me onto his lap and tell me the stories of Achilles, Odysseus, and the gods of Olympus.

I sailed through the assignments, pulling the answers from memory rather than research. Our teacher, Mizz Butcher, decided that we would have a Grecian Feast, complete with seemingly authentic food (brought from our homes), costumes (we each got to pick a character), and most importantly, it would last for two class periods.

Naturally, I chose one of the Olympian gods for my costume, and I wasted no time once I got home in putting it together. I had been assigned olives as the food I was supposed to bring, and while I had never tasted them before, I knew they were a staple of Greek life.

The morning of the celebration was, at last, upon us. I arrived at school extra early. Mizz Butcher was not in her room when I got there, but I would not be distracted. I set my belongings down, and was already starting to put on my costume when my teacher walked through the door.

Her eyes froze on me, her apprehension detectable even behind the glasses she wore. She asked me to come with her, indicating not the classroom door, but instead the door to the closet. When I got into the closet, my eyes landed on a desk and a chair, obviously pulled in there recently. My heart began to speed up. I began to shake.

"Sweetie, you can't come to the celebration."

I must have misheard her. Perhaps, Mizz Butcher had that disease that makes you say things without knowing you were saying them. (I had seen someone who obviously suffered from this condition at a restaurant a few weeks earlier, and pointed to her so I could show my mother. Mother pushed my arm down and was Not Happy for the remainder of the evening).

"You didn't bring back that note that your parent was to sign, and without it, I can't let you come to the celebration." Tears begin to spill down my cheeks; I cannot stop them. "It breaks my heart that the best student in this subject won't be able to partake."

While a classroom party may not seem like much to the more affluent, to step into the roles that I had loved for more than half of my life was better than the promised trip to the spinning Sun Dial Restaurant, located high above Atlanta, if I were to make the honor roll that year.

Perhaps Missus Snave was not too far off the mark when she pinned the notes to my shirt.

Mizz Butcher goes back out to the rest of the students, and I find myself once again in a Tower. While much larger than my previous one, it is still isolation, it is seclusion, and just like Sweet Stream Elementary School, where I could hear the laughter and the shenanigans from the lunchroom, in this Tower I am forced to endure the sounds of my classmates playing and re-enacting scenes that I would love to join. Instead, I sit in the Tower, my costume hanging from a hook over my head, a jar of olives unopened on a shelf, right next to my mother's crystal serving bowl.

For the rest of my life, I will never be able to eat an olive. Unbeknownst to me now, I will wave off proffers with a complaint about the sodium content, and while my adult beverage of choice will one day be a vodka martini, I always opt for a twist. Because of this day, the mere sight of an olive will return me, regardless of age or experience, to the age of eleven, once again locked in a Tower, trying to shut out the sound of my classmates' revelry while at the same time straining to hear, to take part.

I want to be included.

I am released from captivity a couple of hours later, and once again routine resumes its rhythmic rule of my life. My classmates have transformed from the gods and heroes of old back into the uniformed students I knew, ready for the day's next lesson. The incident at Sweet Stream, along with the incident at Wormwood, fades into memory, only to be recalled occasionally over the years.

Two years later, my two Towers collided. I was on the eighth-grade football team at Wormwood, playing center in theory, but bench-warmer in reality. We were at an away game, playing the namesake school of the tiny hamlet east of Atlanta where I had once gone to school. One of the men who held the first down markers came over to me. As I looked into his bright eyes, tucked in the folds of a now-friendly face, I was shocked to find Mr. Welly, the principal of Sweet Stream Elementary School during my brief tenure there, looking back at me. Pleasantries were exchanged; small talk ensued. Minutes later, I was back amongst my teammates, and he had moved further down the field, because despite our daily practices, the other team was better.

I wonder what, if anything, he thought of that encounter. Did he ever realize that, at the behest and with the assistance of Missus Snave, he adjusted the course my life would take, simply by shutting me away with only the King of Scotland and Prince of Denmark to keep me company? Did he ever find missing some of the toys from the Halloween carnival, or realize the off-season appearance of those missing toys coincided with my confinement in my very first Tower? Or was I simply another student labeled "hyperactive" and "gifted", yet punished when I would not conform to the *status quo*?

To be perfectly honest, I walked away from the encounter with only one thought:

As it turned out, the Big Man in the Big Office who, at Missus Snave's command, put me in the Little Closet was now shorter than me.

The
Ugly Duckling

I AM NINETEEN YEARS OLD, and I am freezing my ass off in the middle of the Mediterranean Sea.

Mind you, I am not adrift in an inflatable raft as a result of some catastrophe, nor am I attempting to swim some record-setting distance. Instead, I find myself topside on a guided missile cruiser as she makes her way north toward the Italian port town of Trieste, at the northern-most reach of the Adriatic Sea. It is January, and while magazines and travel guides always paint the Mediterranean as a tropical and exotic paradise, the photographers clearly had never ventured to this particular stretch of water during this time of the year. The winds, which come screaming off the Alps at over fifty miles per hour, efficiently carry an icy chill straight out onto the water. It is that chill which cuts through my pea coat, my uniform, my skin, and seems to be freezing my bones themselves.

God, I wish I had never started smoking. Otherwise, I wouldn't be out here freezing. Instead, I would be back inside the ship, watching one of my shipmates play *Doom* for hours on end.

When I had enlisted with the United States Navy, it had been meant as a way to reboot my life. Much like the computers that were, sometimes, my only friends during my youth, it became necessary from time to time to just clear the cache, stop the processor, and begin to move in a different direction.

During my sophomore year in a small, state college just west of Atlanta, I found that my coursework was not up to "usual" standards, also known as "what my parents expected in return for their investment." It was not the difficulty of the work that was at issue; in fact, it was quite easy compared to what had been assigned to me during my tenure at Wormwood Academy. I simply lacked not only the drive to excel, but in some cases, the drive to simply attend class.

I would later learn exactly how much my parents sacrificed in order to ensure that I would never have to spend another week in the Tower as I had at Sweet Stream. They gave up their money, their home, and their plans for a quiet spot in the country to move to the slowly gentrifying neighborhood in south Atlanta where Wormwood was located. In return, I was expected to study and do my best. While every school year began with a renewed dedication to the goal, each year my resolve was weaker and weaker.

By the time I moved out and went to college, that resolve had all but completely disappeared. It seemed that each "fresh start" I would make began further and further away from the ultimate goal, making the road that much longer, the journey that much more difficult, and the whole endeavor that much more destined to fail.

The siren which called to me, which led me astray, was neither drugs nor alcohol. Nor was it the allure of the opposite sex. By the time I graduated from Wormwood, I had all but surrendered to the fact that my romantic inclinations would always have a more masculine slant.

The proverbial chink in my armor was one that all youths struggle with at some time during their growth: to belong.

Counselors, teachers (both secular and Sunday School), and friends often made reference to the tale of the Ugly Duckling when I was growing up. While I know that their intentions were nothing but noble, I often wonder if they realized exactly how useless that comparison was for me.

To advise a child his their flaws, whether physical or social, will magically melt away upon maturity is too incredulous to all but the most dense of children. Most children can easily extrapolate the intended result: the child will, without effort or sacrifice on his part, become more beautiful than his counterparts, and those who excluded him will have no other option than to shamefully admit his superiority.

Why is the solution to a lack of social integration a promise that the outcast will, one day, reign over his peers?

The ship rocks back and forth through the water, startling me out of my reverie while simultaneously lulling most of the ship's complement to sleep in the decks beneath my feet. I am currently assigned to the midnight shift, and in all honesty, I find I prefer the night. At night, it is hard to see that there is no one else there.

During my days at Wormwood, I had always operated around the lower rungs of the social hierarchy. I may have aspired to be the best and the brightest, but whether due to some physical imperfection, or the fact that I just never understood the mechanics of how to properly integrate myself socially, I never quite seemed to fit in.

When I was in fifth grade, I stayed up late the night before the first Out-Of-Uniform Day that I was to enjoy. While at nine years old I could not even define "fashion sense," nor discern that I did not possess any of the same, I still chose with care my first non-uniform outfit for my new school. The next morning, I donned brown denim pants, a beige-and-brown plaid shirt (complete with mother-of-pearl snap closures), and a brown denim vest which matched the jeans perfectly. My cowboy boots were less comfortable than the black loafers that I normally wore, but I guess that was the price I had to pay for fashion.

Apparently, I had not paid enough.

Within half an hour after arriving at school, I had endured so many jeers and insults I spent my time between classes trying to figure out if I could actually fit myself in my locker, whether or not I could permanently lock myself inside, and if this would, in the long run, be a bad thing.

Over the course of the next eight years, I remained a target. On a middle school science club trip, I found myself sharing a bowling lane with my exotically attractive computer teacher, my science teacher and his fanatical dedication to the Georgia Institute of Technology, and his five-year-old son, while my counterparts enjoyed competing together. During a high school band trip to England, I wound up touring and dining with the chaperones rather than the other students.

I was the outcast who could not even find camaraderie with the other outcasts.

College was much of the same, and without my parents in the next room to forcing me to return to my classes, I soon withdrew completely into my dormitory. I chased off my roommate in the span of three months, and from that point forward lived in another Tower, this time by my own design. My grades fell, my direction began to blur, and before I knew it, I was out of school, crashing with one of the instructors in hastily made plans to avoid returning home.

As fortune would have it, my father's office was the halfway point between my makeshift home and my parents' house, and I would occasionally meet him for lunch. During one of these stilted, awkward conversations, I let slip that I had entertained thoughts of leaving school so I could go work for Carnival Cruise Lines, further misspending my youth by floating around the Caribbean. He suggested that if I really wanted to be on a ship, I should give the Navy a try.

It should not have surprised me that I would go to work the next evening only to find a Naval recruiter sitting at my bar. I will never forget the look in my mother's eyes when I appeared, uninvited, for dinner one night, having spent all day at the Richard B. Russell Federal Building downtown. Her first question ("Did you sign anything?") was quickly followed by her second ("Where did you get a crazy idea like this one?"). As Orwellian as the Federal Building appeared, it was my mother who was beginning to act like Big Brother.

I learned later that my father slept on the couch for a full month after I revealed his involvement in my enlistment.

Staring out at the black veil which surrounds the ship, I shudder into my wool pea coat, and head back down the port side toward the hatch, once more to the cocoon of warmth found inside the skin of the ship. I find my way to the lower decks, and crawl into my rack, pulling the curtain to keep out the light. Sleep soon overtakes me, but my dreams are unsettled. I can hear the guy across from me coming and going, sense his eyes slipping into the space where I sleep, watching me.

I did not know it at the time, but in a month I would need to reinvent myself again. I would be unceremoniously shipped back to the United States, condemned for something that is no longer a crime. I would be stripped of my rank, my privilege, my identity, my security.

Cowboy... Student... Musician... Actor...

I would rekindle a friendship I had held onto since high school, and be whisked to the mountains of east Tennessee. I would be taken to meet people who saw past the feathers, and looked instead at the duck. One of these friendships would last two months, one would still be going strong after two decades.

Student... Sailor... Victim...

I would garner the courage to not merely come out of my proverbial closet, but to also realize that "gay," "smart," "funny," "reliable," and even "ugly" are each only single feathers in the whole coat.

Son... Uncle... Friend... Confidant...

In the end, I would learn that it is simply finding comfort my own imperfect feathers that gave you the elegance and confidence reminiscent of a swan.

INDERELLA

I AM TWENTY-TWO YEARS OLD, and I am standing in dirty, filthy water up to my ankles.

My naval career, having come to an abrupt halt, is fading further and further into my memory. I find myself back in Atlanta, although the city of my youth is nowhere to be found. In the few short years that I was away, the Empire City of the South underwent a myriad of changes, all brought about by one single sentence.

"The International Olympic Committee has awarded the 1996 Olympic Games to the City of Atlanta."

When Juan Antonio Samaranch said those words in the wee hours on a September morning in 1990, the city went insane. As I left Wormwood Academy for the rolling countryside of Carrollton for a quick year of college, construction had already begun. At that time, the only outward signs of the impending changes were merely traffic delays and a massive amount of red Georgia clay scattered everywhere.

When I returned in the early months of 1996, however, the cityscape had changed completely. Skyscrapers had shot up from downtown to Midtown to Buckhead. Streets were oddly clear of panhandlers and debris, the flotsam and jetsam of urban life. Trees had sprung up in neat little rows alongside roads where before there were only bare, broken concrete sidewalks. Green spaces had mysteriously grown out of the urban tableau of chrome and steel and concrete, dappling the city with their verdant patches, miraculously maintained despite the smog and pollution of a million cars.

As I've said before, this was not the city of my youth; this city is now a stranger to me.

Quickly, I find a job tending bar in an Italian restaurant located, not in the tony Buckhead restaurant district, but in the suburb of Tucker, miles to the northeast of all the action. It is somewhat close to my home in Decatur, and the money was good, given the location. I have hardly any expenses of which to speak, and with my grandparents providing room and board, as well as money for fuel and food, I could finally afford to pour resources into my social life.

But once again, just like at Wormwood Academy years before, I find myself looking in on society from the outside, only this time the scale has grown to encompass the entire city rather than simply a school. The heart of the society that I watch, but never dare to fully enter, is called, appropriately, Midtown.

Located between Ponce de Leon Avenue and 24th or 26th streets, depending to whom you ask, this district does not find itself immune from the great transformation in preparation for the Olympics. Once a lair for the less than savory purveyors of theft, assault, and other nefarious actions, Midtown now holds bars, bookstores, a few low-rent apartment buildings, more and more high-dollar homes, twenty-four-hour nightclubs, long-standing Baptist churches, bathhouses, strip clubs, and sex stores—all seemingly within walking distance of each other.

Whether due to the upcoming Games or in spite of them, Atlanta continues to grow exponentially. The metropolis has begun to develop pockets with distinct personalities, traits that are shared not only by the residents, but also the businesses and overall atmosphere of the neighborhood. Little Five Points, a faint echo of New York's Greenwich Village, is relaxed and Bohemian, where one can either sip a latte, have their nipples pierced, or both, depending on their mood. Buckhead drips superficiality and passive aggression, and Decatur is beginning to take on definite Sapphic overtones.

Midtown, however, is able to pull from all walks of life. Every person, from BMW-wielding urban professionals to alternatively employed minimum-wage earners, seems to find a home in those twenty-something blocks in the heart of the city.

How else does the First Baptist Church of Atlanta wind up four lanes of traffic away from the largest gay bar in town?

As with Wormwood, my observation of Midtown begins ostensibly from without, never straying too far within its boundaries, never fully quenching the thirst to belong. I drive my pickup truck, new when Reagan was in office, into town searching for something – anything – but always find myself driving home, still wanting. I work in a restaurant, and not even a good one at that. I am neither a doctor, nor a lawyer, nor an Indian chief, and while I long to be one of the shiny, happy people, I can never seem to polish up the right way.

I had never stopped to wonder if I was the only person who found fault with my situation. Nor have I considered the quality of person who would find fault with someone's socioeconomic status, be it greater or lesser than their own.

"*Caliente!*" cries one of the cooks, snapping me out of my reverie, and slamming a pan on the flat metal surface of the dish pit—my home for the evening as I work off some transgression I have committed, but cannot remember.

"You do know I'm not Mexican, right?" I call after him, but his attention is already onto the next thing. I return my focus to the recently-deposited saucepan caked with the detritus of the remnants of the dinner shift. My stomach lurches as a grotesquely burned shrimp, a refugee from a primavera long gone, clings desperately to the edge of the pan. Sighing, I grab a piece of steel wool and get to work. Despite being relegated to the dish pit for some sin committed in my manager's eyes, I have grown to appreciate the solitude of my new situation. I do not have to gracefully endure the good-meaning, yet ill-educated customers asking for *Fuh-tuck-anny Al-freddo* in a vain attempt to properly pronounce the dish's name, nor must I endure the whining of my co-workers because they have to bring more bread to a table of six who ordered the Eternal Salad and Soup combination. It always amazes me how people could expect so much for doing so little.

Just after closing, one of the servers, Adam, sticks his balding head under the glass racks and informs me that he and a couple of other servers are going across the street to unwind at the bar which stays open until two in the morning. The invitation startles me; I had never been asked to join the nightly outing before tonight. As expected, the second I decide to join them, the kitchen staff deposits their tools from the evening on the stainless steel shelf that is my responsibility.

Shit.

Nearly an hour later when I walk out of the restaurant, only the manager is left behind me. Every muscle in my body complains as I climb into my aged Ford pickup truck and start the engine, my eyes drifting across the intersection to the small cluster of restaurants found there. I can easily read the green neon spelling out "O'Malley's," and I can also see the dented top of Adam's ancient Honda Accord – new before I was even in high school. What the hell? I can always go to sleep later if the evening turns out to be a bust.

I push open the heavy oak doors of O'Malley's only to find the place deserted, my co-workers gone. Adam must have left his car here, and, given what I know of his drinking habits, that was probably a wise decision. In fact, the bar seems to be completely devoid of any human life, the only noise coming from the shiny, brand-new jukebox that sits in the corner, looking even more out of place than I feel. Having realized that my hopes of social integration would have to wait for another time, I turn to leave, only to be stopped by the sound of a swinging door and the purr of a gentle voice.

"Come on, now, don't run away. Otherwise I'm gonna be stuck here for the next two hours by myself, and there's only so much CNN a girl can watch."

I do not know why I turn around, but the sight that greets me when I do is not anything close to what I was expecting. Given the part of town, the lateness of the hour, and the fact that it is a Wednesday night, I fully expected a well-worn woman to be tending the bar in this dive.

Instead, standing before me is one of the most beautiful women I have ever beheld. Tall and leggy, her blond hair cascades in waves down her back, held away from her face by a simple black band. Her features are delicate, as are her arms, looking diminutive next to the case of beer she is carrying.

"Um, okay." I answer, not sure where I found my voice.

"Excellent," she replies, sitting the beer on the bar, all the while looking directly into my eyes. Her eyes are sky blue, and while they are as delicate as the rest of her form, behind them simmers an intensity that seems to be too big for her body.

"Sit," she says, gesturing toward a barstool with her chin. While only one word has been spoken aloud, I can hear an entire paragraph behind it. "Take a seat if you wish," she seems to say, "though once you do there is no turning back."

This woman is truly a mystery.

I slip onto a black, fake-leather barstool, mended in three places with dull, gray duct tape, the edges turned up and black with grime. Not knowing what else to do, I tap my fingers nervously on the bar. Once again, I am under her stare, but this time it is more questioning, searching. If I didn't know any better, I could have sworn she was trying to analyze me.

"You're having a vodka cranberry," she states simply. Apparently I do not have a choice in the matter. Before I can respond, she turns her back to me, and I hear the telltale clink of ice being dropped into a glass, followed quickly by a nearly silent splash of liquid.

"Don't you mean a Cape Cod?" I ask.

"If I had meant a Cape Cod, I would have said a Cape Cod. Besides, I haven't decided if you're worth it for me to cut up limes." In a single, fluid motion, she turns around and sits the cocktail before me—no napkin, no straw. I take a tentative sip, the warmth of the vodka spreading throughout my mouth, followed quickly by the tart crispness of the cranberry. Swallowing, I choked slightly on the burning taste of the alcohol.

Holding the glass up to the light, I immediately realized why.

She has not made a drink that resembles fruit punch. Instead, it looks as if she has simply filled the glass with vodka, then told it a naughty joke, causing it to blush ever so slightly.

"Too strong for you?"

"No," I rasp. "Just not used to having them made... this way."

"Well, that's your first problem," she said, smirking the entire time. "You've never had a decent drink before."

"My name is..."

"I know who you are," she says. "You're the gay guy from Napoleano's, across the street. You just moved back to town, from somewhere up north, and everyone thinks you're either the quietest person ever invented, or you're secretly plotting to blow up the restaurant." It amazes me the way she speaks, seemingly without a need to pause for a breath. "For the record, they're divided on whether or not blowing up the restaurant is a good thing or a bad thing, in case that's what you're actually doing."

"And if I am?" I ask, attempting coyness.

"Make sure you don't get caught," she retorts, smoothly. "Oh, and stop trying to be coy. You're not good at it."

She would eventually give me her name, but whether it was her slender build or her pale, delicate features hiding an Olympian strength, I would always know her as "Artemis."

Again, I am stunned into silence. I begin to think that I should probably stay quiet, but quickly abandon that thought, asking instead about my co-workers' whereabouts.

"Your friends went down to Maggie's; apparently things aren't happening enough here."

Immediately, I find myself insulted on her behalf. I do not know why, but I already feel an ever-so-slight, yet quickly growing bond with this woman.

"Are you going to join them?"

Her question hangs in the air, and while we have only just met, and though it is probably nothing more than Artemis wondering if she should cash me out now, or open a tab, I have the feeling that I stand at a crossroads. Eventually, I will have to figure out how I came to this particular juncture, but for the time being, my response is nearly immediate, and shockingly honest.

"You versus those assholes?" I ask, rhetorically. "No contest."

She smiles. It is a small smile, just a quirky upturn of the corners of her lips, but it reaches all the way to her eyes, which now seems to flash with earnestness and mischievousness all at the same time.

"I knew you weren't the complete loser they said you were" she says, plucking a beer from the cooler and twisting the top off, tossing the metal disk into a trash can over her shoulder without even looking. She takes a quick sip and holds it in her mouth, her ice-blue eyes once again appraising me. I lower my head under her stare, and am shocked when I feel her fingers on my chin. She lifts my head and looks me square in the eye.

"Sweetie, we don't look at our drinks when I'm behind the bar. I didn't go to all this effort getting pretty so you could stare at ice in a glass."

I stay until closing, and then we part ways in the parking lot, despite my proffer for breakfast at the 24-hour diner around the corner. I am elated the entire drive home, and as I roll into the driveway (my headlights off so not to disturb my grandparents' slumber), I know that I made the right choice by staying. With Artemis, anything seems possible, and the citizens of Atlanta would do well to take care.

Bonnie had met Clyde.

While I wouldn't characterize our friendship as "inseparable," Artemis and I are as thick as thieves. I become a late night fixture at O'Malley's, but only on the nights that she is working. I always sit at the corner of the bar, nearly hiding behind one of the corner supports, never really interacting with anyone until most of the patrons have gone, and she and I have the place to ourselves. Late nights are quickly augmented with lunches, errand-running, movie dates, and just general companionship. It is the first time in years that I have, simply put, a friend.

To have a companion free of romantic, professional, financial or familial entanglements is a salve to my sore soul. I have learned all too well that most interpersonal relationships come with the proverbial attached strings, so in the end, I feel as if I am nothing more than a marionette.

My friendship with Artemis is a refreshing respite from this all-but-universal truth.

I rapidly grow to trust this woman, this muse, this goddess. Honestly, she never really gave me a choice. I can tell her anything. Whether it is an artifact of her personality, or simply one of the side-effects of working behind a bar for years, she rarely holds back when it comes time to advise on what I should do, what I should have done, and what would have happened if she had been there in the first place.

Artemis meets most of my family, and most of them love her. She becomes my "beard," and I am her "G.B.F." a decade before the term will become part of the social lexicon. She confides that she loves going out with me in part because she can wear the big, chunky heels which raise her height to over six-feet-four-inches. She cannot normally wear her beloved stilts when she is on a date with one of her numerous suitors, as they tend to take issue with being shorter than she.

It is a good thing she usually sends them packing early in the process; if they were to stick around, they would soon discover that her height is only the beginning.

Our friendship, however, is not rooted in our social life. As we grow closer and closer together, our relationship deepens even further, and she soon has unfettered access to the darkest, most private corners of my life: the part of my soul that I freely give to those who claim to love me.

She knows that I moved home fresh on the heels of a very intense breakup with a guy who would soon be referred to simply as "Sneezy." And in spite of (or in testament to) the purity and strength of our connection, she does not allow me to wallow for very long.

I deduce this last point shortly after a filthy bar rag strikes me fully in the face. When it falls off, I see Artemis behind the bar, hands on her hips, once again her intense gaze turned my way, staring neither into my face nor into my eyes.

This time, she stares directly into my soul.

If I am being completely truthful, when she looks at me in this moment, I want nothing more than to leap from my seat, and run out the front door of the bar. I even give it thirty seconds or so of consideration, the muscles in my legs tensing in preparation to flee. I realize quickly, however, that Artemis would simply tackle me in the parking lot, drag me back inside, sit me back down in my chair, and make me talk anyway. If I stay where I am, there will be less physical injury.

"What?" I ask, defensively.

"Who is he?"

"Who is who?"

"Who is the guy," she elaborated, "that has you sitting at the corner of my bar looking like a broken-winged bird almost every night after work? When we go out, or you come here, you might have your mask in place, but I can still see that you're in pain. When you think no one is looking, when you think you're not being observed—that is when the mask starts to slip. So I want to know: Whose ass do I have to whip?"

Damn her and her insight.

"Careful, darling," I drawl in my best Southern accent. "Your slip is showing."

"And I don't care," she retorts, before I can hide behind another euphemism. "Details. Now."

Once I begin to tell the tale, however, something interesting occurs. The more I talk about it, the more I wanted to talk about it, until the whole of the story gushes from me like the water that pours out of a faucet when you twist the knob so hard it snaps off in your hand. Through the entire story, Artemis stands perfectly still, her back straight, her shoulders squared, and her entire focus on me.

I speak of deception and manipulation, of desperation and fear. I speak of the blackness that threatens to consume me daily. If a degenerate sociopath like Sneezy could toss me aside so easily, what was to stop everyone else to whom I would give my heart from doing the exact same thing?

Love is a force with which to be reckoned; it empowers as it weakens, energizes as it exhausts. There are no laws or rules to which it will submit, nor do you get out of it what you put into it. Sometimes, you receive your investment back tenfold, while sometimes you simply receive nothing, or worse, it costs you more than you bargained. It clouds the mind, confuses the ability to reason, and encourages us to try things we never would have even considered before Eros fired his arrow into your heart.

Of all the emotions in the world, only love possesses the duality to both break and mend a heart.

"And that's how I got… here," I hear myself saying, as if I were listening to the story rather than telling it. "I called my mother, she bought me a bus ticket from Wisconsin to Atlanta, and informed me that, while she could afford a plane ticket, I really needed to take the 26-hour bus ride to think about the direction my life was headed."

"You may have thought your mom was a bitch," Artemis states precisely, "but she had a point."

I begin to ramble about how Sneezy and I are meant to be together, and how we would fix everything, and that this is only a temporary break.

"You're an idiot. Apparently those twenty-six hours did nothing."

"Wait just a damn minute. I might be a sap, a romantic, a... I might be a lot of things, but I am not an idiot. I went to Wormwood Academy, after all."

"So what?" she says. "Just because you know how to split atoms or cure cancer doesn't mean that you're not an idiot when it comes to real life."

I sit there, simultaneously wounded by her words, but also soothed by her concern for me. Artemis looks at me for a long minute, and when she speaks next, her voice is lower and softer, but still just as passionate as a moment ago.

"You're an idiot, but you're a special kind of idiot," she says, walking over and taking my hands in hers. Despite being in ice half the night while fixing drinks, her hands always feel warm to me. "You're *my* idiot. You and Sneezy are not going to get back together; he asked you to move eight states away. You might see him once, maybe twice before you die. He's not worth your time, and he sure as hell ain't worth mine."

Her last little declaration echoes through the room, which is now devoid of human life save ourselves, almost daring me to move on with my life, to try new things, to... go to Midtown?

"You hurt because you're growing," she said, returning to her nightly cleaning of the bar. "But no one said you had to grow every day. Would you like to see what all is out there? I bet there is a big difference between the men here and… where was it you met Sneezy? Wisconsin?"

"We lived in Wisconsin toward the end," I reply, my voice faltering on the word "end." It is the first time I have ever used such a finite term to describe my relationship. "But we met in Norfolk, Virginia. We were both stationed there."

"Would you like to see what Atlanta has to offer?"

I nod.

"Excellent. It's much easier when you agree with me from the start. There's less physical injury." She leans against the beer cooler opposite from where I sit, crossing her long legs at the ankle, and begins to look me up and down. "Although, we're probably going to need to get you some new clothes first."

This earns her an eye roll.

It takes a couple of weeks for our schedules to align so we both have the same, consecutive Friday, Saturday and Sunday off of work. In the hospitality industry, one does not eschew a weekend dinner shift due to its increased earning potential. Taking Sunday off is done as a precaution, according to Artemis.

"Just in case," she says.

"In case of what?" I ask.

"In case you decide to deplete the vodka supply in Atlanta six ounces at a time. I almost regret introducing you to the martini. Although, I still insist that a proper martini is prepared with olives."

"No olives," I reply firmly. "Ever."

After we both close our respective restaurants on Thursday, we venture back to her place. She has a two-bedroom apartment, and after pulling four double-shifts in a row, I want nothing more than to crawl into bed for half a day. As with most things in my life, it is simply not meant to be. She wakes me up at some ungodly hour before lunchtime, and tells me to get cleaned up, then dressed to go out.

"Are there clubs open this early?" I groggily ask.

"Yes, one. But you generally don't go there at eleven a.m. You might leave it at eleven a.m., but you don't go there at eleven a.m." I had always wondered why she had four pairs of sunglasses in her car at all times.

Artemis sits at an old wooden dining table, ringed with chairs that match neither the table nor each other. Her legs are pulled up to her chest and she sips a cup of coffee. A second cup rests on the table, next to the comics from last Sunday's paper.

"Drink your coffee and wake up a little bit, darling. We've got a full day ahead of us, so we'll stop for breakfast on our way to Lenox." I am actually surprised at her choice of shopping centers; while there are at least three between her apartment and the middle of Buckhead, Lenox Square Mall offers more diversity amongst its four levels of shops than Northlake or North Dekalb. I sit and sip, shocked that she remembers how I like my coffee – black with enough sugar to send a diabetic into a coma. I hold up the comics and look at her.

"I didn't know what part of the paper you would want," she answers the question asked silently by my single, raised eyebrow. "But everyone loves the funny papers."

We drink our coffee and read our papers, and the only sounds in the house are the occasional turn of a page, or the soft clunk of a cup being set down on the table. Her voice startles me when she suddenly begins barking orders.

"Now hurry up, you still need to change."

"Can't I just go like this?" I ask. She was just starting to get up from her chair when my words freeze her mid-rise. She slowly turns her head toward me, and looks at me, slowly and deliberately, from the top of my head to the bottom of my shoes.

Standing fully, she reaches out and slips her hand over mine, giving it a reassuring squeeze as she leans nearer and nearer, her lips drawing close to my ear.

"Sweetie," she stage-whispers, "the fact that you think it acceptable to go out looking like that is the whole reason we're going shopping."

Shopping, amazingly, is actually enjoyable. We spend most of the day at it, with frequent breaks for food, coffee, and a cocktail or two. When it is over, I have purchased enough Artemis-approved clothing to last a month of Saturday nights, although she merely graces me with a slightly-snobbish "It's a start."

Back at her place, we toss *Casablanca* in the VCR, and open a bottle of red wine. I pick out what I will wear that night when we venture into town.

"The jeans from Macy's, the shirt from Structure, and the new black slip-on shoes," she calls out after me.

Seriously?

"What, no advice on my underwear?"

"You only bought one pair – not really much of a choice there."

Artemis makes a simple meal out of chicken, potatoes, and some green vegetable that I have no intention of eating. She does me the courtesy of not even putting it on my plate, and as we finish up dinner and drain the last of the merlot, I finally ask the question I have avoided all day.

"Where are we going tonight?"

"Midtown," she replies.

"I know, but where in Midtown?" I honestly want to know. I had ventured out on my own a time or two, but always without success.

How does one define success when visiting a bar alone?

"We'll go into Backstreet and at least get our hands stamped so we don't have to wait in that god-awful line later on," she says. On a couple of weekend nights I had actually plucked up the courage to go over to the twenty-four-hour gay bar that squatted on almost an entire block, and I could personally attest to the slow-moving chain of people waiting their turn to enter the establishment. "If you want to go hunting, sometimes it's just easier to start at the watering hole. Now, go get dressed. The Jimmies will be here soon."

"What are Jimmies?" This is the first I have heard of them.

"My friends Jimmy and Jimmy. You know… the Jimmies." She stares at me as if this is explanation enough, and on a night when I am trying new things, I find it perfectly satisfactory.

I quickly change into the clothes that Artemis had dictated, and before I have a chance to turn coward, a horn blows outside. Artemis opens the door, makes some sort of spastic gesture that, I think, translates to "we're almost ready, don't bother coming in, we'll be out in just a second, and do you mind turning that damn music down?" Without shutting the door, she turns to me, and, not for the first time, my breath catches in my throat.

In a misguided attempt to blend into the background, Artemis has chosen a black cocktail dress with a hemline that dares a man's eyes to travel further up her legs than would normally be socially acceptable. She wears her hair loose, blonde waves falling over one bare shoulder and settling on her bosom, the off-the-shoulder dress allowing for only the smallest hint of cleavage. I cannot name the fabric, but it is so black that it seems to absorb the light itself, reflecting nothing back.

"Dude," she says, impatiently. "My eyes are up here."

Suddenly realizing my *faux pas*, I quickly lift my head, only to be struck dumb once more. Her head is in perfect alignment with the streetlight outside her apartment building. The amber glow of the streetlight radiates from behind her, not enhancing her beauty but simply accenting the perfection which is already there.

"Now," she says, reaching forward and taking my hand, "get in the damn carriage Cinderella. This Fairy Godmother is going to the ball with you."

Neither of us makes it home until after dinner on Sunday night. Artemis stays by my side the entire time, and I very quickly learn that she possesses the one skill that I still find lacking in my arsenal: courage. Despite my proficiency in other subjects, when it came to social skills, I am the slowest of students. However, Artemis is a patient teacher, and soon I was am forth on my own into those no-longer-daunting numbered streets in the heart of Atlanta. My decisions range from the good, to the bad, to the ugly, and while I may never find my Prince Charming in the public houses of Atlanta, I do find my share of friends, paramours, boyfriends, lovers, teachers, students, confidants, enemies, liars, cheaters and thieves.

One night, years later, Artemis and I descend once more upon Midtown. We have just turned the corner at 10th Street and Piedmont Avenue, where the porch of Outwrite Bookstore & Coffee Shop is crowded to overflowing with the eighteen-to-twenty-one crowd. I can feel someone's eyes on me, so I stop and turn to face Artemis, allowing for a slightly better view of the occupants of the porch.

As usual, no one is looking at me.

In fact, the only person I can see clearly is sitting, facing away from me, on the red metal railing, his tank top riding up just enough to show the hieroglyph tattoo in the small of his back: the eye of Horus, the protector.

Shrugging it off, we resume our journey to Blake's On The Park, only to stop again, this time both of us looking at our reflections in the plate glass of the front windows, our bodies superimposed on the flurry of activity within the bar.

"Ready to go hunting?" she asks.

"Not tonight," I say, fishing my driver's license out of the pocket of my jeans. "But I will buy my Fairy Godmother a well-earned drink."

She hooks a slender arm through my own, and leans in close to whisper in my ear.

"Well-earned is perfectly fine," she says, her voice low but firm. "But well brand is simply unacceptable."

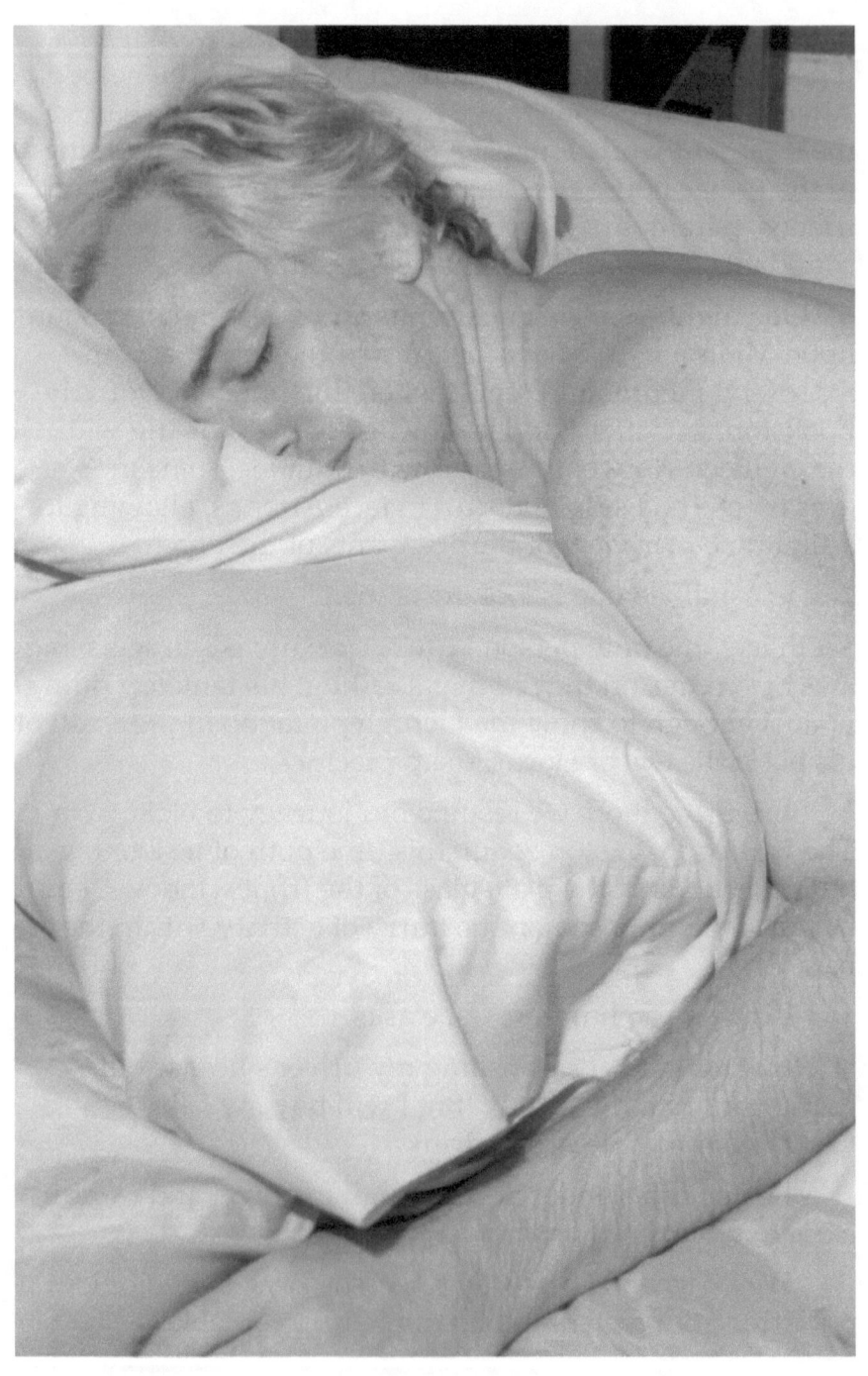

 Sleeping Beauty

I AM THIRTY-SIX YEARS OLD, and I feel as if I have been sleeping for thirty-five of those years.

Not "sleeping" in the literal sense, as I am neither emaciated, nor atrophied, nor the subject of a story on the front page of *The National Enquirer*. I have neither succumbed to a witch's spell, nor have I taken all the Valium available on the W.A.S.P. Country Club Circuit on which I had been raised. Instead, I have been asleep in a more metaphoric sense, dream-walking my way through my own life, never really reaching, never really stretching, never really risking pain and suffering.

This is not to say that I have never taken chances or acted impulsively. I have opened myself up to what I believed to be love and in return, I was hurt, badly. I have made life-changing decisions on a whim. I have fretted endlessly over mundane details that did not require that level of concern.

It was late May of 2011 when the Fates themselves chose to offer me a chance at a better life, should I be wise enough not only to recognize it, but also to take it.

Memorial Day, Labor Day, and other three-day weekends are totally lost on me, as I have neither the means nor the desire to travel anywhere. Nor am I socially adept enough, despite Artemis' patient teachings, to garner an invitation to a barbecue or other such event. Over the years I had cultivated a small group of friends, and while they are fewer in number than many of my contemporaries, the bonds we share were deep, well-founded and permanent. One such person is my colleague, Melinda.

Melinda and I form the Client Services arm of the company for which we both work, charged with maintaining open and effective communications between the firm and its client base. It is a job that we are able to do with varying levels of success. She is my back-up as I am hers, and not a single day goes by that we didn't speak at least once.

It is the Friday before Memorial Day, around ten in the morning, when we both notice that most, if not all, of our clients have chosen to augment the three-day weekend with extra time off. E-mails sit unanswered and phone calls remain unreturned. While Melinda is trapped under a seemingly endless project, I have nothing of importance on my calendar, save my monthly lunch with two of my close friends. My dining plans include Kenneth, with whom I had worked at a previous job, and Narasimha, whom I had known since I was eleven years old. Narasimha lived across the street from where my family had settled in a slowly-gentrifying neighborhood after my acceptance to Wormwood Academy. Narasimha insisted that we call him "Nick," and while I will never understand the translation, I never argued.

Hindi names have a tendency to test even the most eloquent elocution.

We have just placed our orders with the visibly-tattooed server at The Vortex in Little Five Points when I choose to share something with my friends that had been rolling around in my head for quite some time.

"So, I'm going to quit dating," I state. "I'm just… done."

Never having been the luckiest in love, I had persevered, seldom understanding why I always wound up the one being hurt. Einstein defined insanity as "doing the same thing over and over again expecting a different result"; if this is truly the case, when it came to love, I certainly certifiable.

"Well, that's sudden," noted Kenneth, his small, green eyes staring directly at me. Kenneth and I are, on many levels, the same person, which is why we only meet for lunch once each month. Neither of us can stand the other too long or too frequently. "I respect your choice, but it seems a little rushed."

"Is ten years rushed?" I ask, rhetorically. "I mean, I've been out there trying, hoping, wishing, and while I would prefer that this discussion not turn into an episode of *Dr. Phil*, I just think it's time to focus on other things."

"Like what?" asks Nick, his gentle demeanor nudging the conversation along.

"Work, family. I have a niece that must be spoiled relentlessly," I begin, but almost immediately lose the momentum of the statement. I really have not thought this all the way through.

True to form, I have once again based a life-altering decision on an impulse, and find myself at a loss when simply asked about what would take the place of love.

"Honestly, I don't care what you do; it's your life," says Kenneth, who was not well-known for his tact. His directness, however, is an oddly welcome bonus. "You don't want to date? Don't date. You don't want to be with anyone, then don't be with anyone. There's no law that says that everyone has to find someone; lots of people go through their lives without settling down with a partner. Live and let live. All that aside, I do want you to make me one promise."

"And that would be?" I ask. Deals with Kenneth could be tricky, if not outright Faustian in nature. "Do I have to give you my soul?"

"Nope. This is a freebie," he assures me. "Just promise me that if the opportunity arises, if it knocks at your door, you will at least have the good sense to answer it."

"Sure," I say half-heartedly. Even if I try and fail, there is no real way for Kenneth to know, so there is no harm in trying. A church bell in the distance chimes once, sounding oddly out of place among the din of the restaurant.

Our burgers arrive. I take the first bite of my simple cheeseburger—plain with just a slice of pepper jack cheese—and am immediately reminded of the real reason we chose this particular restaurant. It is neither the two-story skull whose gaping mouth forms the front entrance, nor is it the alternative decor (most ostensibly the motorcycle hanging from the ceiling), nor the full page in the menu that lists, quite amusingly, the rules for dining at The Vortex.

It is the simple fact that I could order my burger medium-rare and no one will give me any lip.

Lunch progresses and our conversation meanders through the usual content of politics, sports, current events, sex, relationships, work, more politics, and then more and more of the same. Talking with these two is never forced, always intelligent and more often than not, amusing. Regardless of where one stands on a particular issue, there is no disrespect at our table. Topics are debated openly and thoroughly, but there is never a trace of malice or superiority. My previous pronouncement has been forgotten, and soon I bid Kenneth and Nick farewell, promising to meet them in another month's time.

I am walking the two blocks to my car when my phone rings. It is about time for the daily call with Melinda, so I flip open my phone without even looking at the display.

"Hello, sweetie," I say, a little more sultry than I normally would with a colleague. Then again, Melinda and I, having worked together for so long, are sometimes less-than-perfectly-professional when we spoke. It helped to relieve stress and blow off steam.

To my surprise, it is not Melinda on the phone. Instead, it is the voice of a man who I will later know as Prince Charming.

It should be noted that his parents neither had the last name of Charming, nor did they name him "Prince" in deference to the 80's rock icon. We had courted ever so cautiously online for almost two years when one Sunday afternoon in April, he suggested that we meet.

He had extended numerous invitations previously, but for some reason when he said "come over" that particular evening, I could honestly not find any reason to decline.

We made no plans beyond my picking him up at his place and then "going from there."

U.S. Highway 41 runs from northwest to southeast, bisecting the city of Atlanta nearly straight down the middle. Most people refer to it simply as "41," but it does use other names, including Northside Drive, Cobb Parkway, and Tara Boulevard. As with anything else in metropolitan Atlanta, it all depended, not on where you were going, but where you happened to be at the time.

Prince Charming happened to be in Kennesaw, on the distant northwestern edge of what could reasonably be called metro Atlanta. Even on a Sunday afternoon, that meant a solid forty-five minute drive from my house, south of town, and then we would, as he put it, "go from there."

Prince Charming's directions led me to an nondescript, extended-stay motel right on Cobb Parkway. It was the type of place where the rooms opened directly to the outside, connected by the traditional concrete breezeways, with only a thin, iron railing preventing people from falling over the edge. Air conditioning units stuck out of the walls at regular intervals, some silent, some rattling into the spring twilight as they forced cool air into the rooms they served.

Not knowing where his particular room was located, I parked my aging white Buick Skylark in the front of the motel, where the light from the street lamps was plentiful. The other three sides of the property were walled by trees that had been overgrown by kudzu, its thick foliage forming nearly-solid green towers, blocking all but a few slivers of the rapidly diminishing sunlight.

Some people may have judged Prince Charming based simply on his address. Where one eats, where one sleeps, and where one prays (or even if they choose to pray at all) are often judged, to varying degrees, by their peers, friends, colleagues and family.

Given my background, I should have dutifully become one of these people, these self-appointed judges. If his proffered invitation had come a decade before, I would have driven straight past the motel without even slowing, a fumbling text message my only apology.

An experience years before, however, had taught me a very valuable lesson. I had been in my late twenties, and while I did have a job and transportation, I did not have a steady place to live. After sharing space with several friends, my parents allowed me to move back home for a short while, but that quickly grew tiresome for everyone. Despite my age and overall resemblance to a "responsible adult," I would always possess certain traits that my parents would find inappropriate.

Mother, in an attempt to present a solution alongside the discussion of the problem, had even gone as far as to research the rates and policies at a property similar to the one before which I now stood. My entire adult life, possessions and all, had been reduced to a room with a kitchenette, bathroom en suite, and a semi-functional air conditioner to keep me comfortable. At night, drug dealers and prostitutes would roam the parking lot, and I was kept awake by the loud music and near-constant sound of car engines as the multiple occupants of the multiple rooms in the multiple buildings came and went.

After six weeks at that place, I pulled myself together, got an apartment and a new job, and was soon back on track to what my parents and their peers defined as "success." I would, however, always carry with me, an understanding for those who may have not quite found their path.

While I wandered through my memories, I also wandered the breezeways of this no-tell motel, the muted thuds of my footfalls on the concrete reflecting off all the hard surfaces. Making my way to the second floor, I soon located the correct door, raising my hand to knock.

Before my knuckles could make contact with the door, it was pulled open. Blue eyes stared out at me from the dimly lit room. His eyes perfectly matched his hair, which was cut into a thick Mohawk that stood a full six inches off his scalp. He was slightly taller than me, forcing me to lift my head to look into his eyes. My brain barely registered the tank top and shorts that he wore because of what I saw.

In his deep blue eyes, I could see eternity.

"Hey," he said. "You wanna come in?" He stepped back to allow me entrance.

I could not move. In the distance, I could hear the faint ring of a church bell chiming the hour—six evenly spaced, metallic tones that resonated from one of the seemingly hundreds of steeples that were scattered across the rolling hills of suburban Atlanta.

"Um," I said succinctly, and then without another word, I walked through the door.

If you had asked me a mere five minutes prior to seeing him, not on a computer screen but with my own eyes, whether or not I believed in the overly-romanticized concept of "love at first sight," I would have laughed openly, loudly, and mockingly. Love is not logical, and therefore had no place in my world.

Thirty seconds after I walked through that door, however, my answer had reversed itself completely. We spent the evening together not doing much of anything other than talking and watching a movie. During the film, he incrementally shifted closer and closer to where I sat until our sides were touching, his left hand tentatively reaching for my right. Instinctively, I laced my fingers through his, and we held hands until the credits were crawling up the screen on the flat-panel television that sat on one of the desks in the room.

Neither of us spoke, but instead turned our heads to look at each other, the silence in the room noticeable but comfortable. Once again I was swept into his eyes, unable to look away, locked in a gaze that was so intense that his eyes seemed to be getting bigger.

It wasn't until his lips touched mine that I realized he had been leaning in to kiss me. While it was not a chaste kiss, it was not inappropriate for a first meeting, particularly a first meeting that had taken two years of intense and conversation to bring to bear. Tentative and hesitant at first, our kiss grew bolder and more daring as it progressed. I could feel the air leave my lungs, my breath plucked from me by Prince Charming.

The kiss ended. He leaned his head forward, his forehead coming to rest on my own. I mumbled some offhand comment about needing to get back home, but I knew, more surely than I had known anything in my thirty-six years on this Earth, that leaving his side was the last thing I wanted to do.

He nodded, and then quickly kissed me again. Unlike its predecessor, this kiss seemed perfunctory and quick, lacking the warmth and the passion of the one that came before it. We said our goodbyes, and I left.

As I eased my car into the traffic on Cobb Parkway, turning south to start the long drive back home, I knew that I had felt a connection, nay, a bond between us. I knew that he was the one that I had been seeking, even though throughout that pursuit I never knew who he was. I quickly glanced at my phone on the passenger seat, the silver shape visible in the dark against the burgundy fabric, wanting to call him, even if all I did was hear his voice once more.

I had fallen in love at the first sight of him, and I did what any rational, logic-driven person would have in the same situation: I ran like hell. Prince Charming did not call me again, nor did I attempt to contact him. I returned to the beige rhythm of my soporific life, and I simply assumed that he returned to his.

Six weeks later, on the Friday before Memorial Day, I am driving into the heart of downtown Atlanta, transiting back to my home from my lunch date at The Vortex in Little Five Points. Prince Charming has called, having no plans for the long weekend himself, and asks what I have planned. Shocked into silence, I once again began to stammer the same way I did at his doorway the first, and only, time we had met.

As I head east on I-20, I can see the city skyline looming above me, the grays of the skyscrapers almost blending in with the clouds that fill the sky. The exit for Interstates 75 and 85, both north and south, is coming up, and once again I find myself at a crossroads, this time both literal and proverbial.

To the south is my home, where things are ordered and logical. I have a dog to keep me company, a rescued greyhound named Mercury. I can trace my love for the athletic elegance of the breed back to Speedy, my very first dog as a child. Although she was a melting pot of several breeds, Speedy most resembled a greyhound, that breed which dates back to the days of mythological Egypt. I am friendly with one of my next-door neighbors, and even, occasionally, go out to the Irish Bred Pub, the Brake Pad or the Manchester Arms for a bit of libation and revelry. My parents stop by occasionally, and I have even managed to host my own cook-out almost two years prior on Memorial Day weekend.

To the north, however, is Prince Charming, beautiful and intriguing. I still remember the intensity of our connection, the power behind his first kiss. Unbidden, Kenneth's words slam into my brain so forcibly that I swear I hear his voice in my head:

"If the opportunity arises, if it knocks at your door, you will at least have the good sense to answer it." I silently curse Kenneth as my thumb presses redial on the phone.

"Hello?" answers Prince Charming, confused.

"Hey. Pack three days worth of clothes. Bring whatever you want; we'll figure out what we're doing later."

"Um… um… okay." I have never made anyone stammer before, and I know that I am blushing. I am usually the one who finds himself inarticulate. "Are you sure?" he asks, his tone of voice daring me to say yes.

Who am I to refuse a dare?

"Yes," I say. "I'm thirty minutes away. See you soon."

I end the call and steer my Buick onto the ramp heading north, my heart beating hard and fast, my fingers twitching against the vinyl steering wheel with anxiety and anticipation. As I merge into the highway proper, I suddenly find myself moving at less than twenty miles an hour. Apparently, everyone else in Atlanta has the same idea about blowing off the last half of the day and getting an early start on the weekend.

Dammit.

I quickly call Prince Charming back and let him know that I would be a little late due to traffic. Then I call Melinda, put her on speaker-phone, open the window a few inches, and light a cigarette.

"What are you doing?" she asks.

"Going to pick up somebody," I reply, not wanting to volunteer all the details up front. Artemis is wrong; I can be coy if I try hard enough.

"Quit being coy, you suck at it," is Melinda's assessment. "When you say pick someone up, are you headed to someone's house or are you headed to a bar?"

"I have no idea what you mean," I reply, tossing the cigarette out the window and rolling it up.

"I mean, do you know this person already, or are you heading out in the hopes that you randomly happen upon Mr. Right?"

"I know who he is," I say, shocked at my confidence in that statement. "I'm picking him up at his place, then we're heading back to mine. From there, anything's possible. We might run around all weekend naked, we might hit the road for a quick trip, we might marathon movies the entire time. The possibilities are endless."

"You know, you really should find one person and settle down, like the rest of us had to do," says Melinda. "You're gay and in your thirties. Maybe it's time to play a little less 'hard-to-get' and a little more 'beat-the-clock'."

"You can be a real bitch sometimes. You know that, right?" I ask, the question entirely rhetorical.

"Yes, my ex-husband was quite clear about that fact," she retorts. "But, you know I'm right."

"Listen," I say, "if God wants me to settle down, he is more than welcome to find the perfect person for me and drop him in my lap, all wrapped up with a pretty little bow. But until that day comes, I'm not going to be sitting on my laurels."

She is still laughing when we end the call, as I was passing Mount Paran Road, the megalithic church of the same name clearly visible from the highway. The church's bells chimed four times as I slowly crept past in traffic that was gruesome, even by Atlanta standards.

As I pull into the back parking lot of the motel that Prince Charming calls home, I am shocked to find him waiting for me outside, a gym bag over one shoulder, and two binders cradled to his chest. He opens the back door, drops the binders and his bag on the back seat, then lets himself into the front of the car, the heavy white door swinging shut behind him. I look at him, thrilled that our previous encounter had not been a freak accident, elated that he is, once again, close to me. Glancing at the binders in the backseat, I raise one eyebrow questioningly.

"DVDs," is his hesitant reply. I say nothing, but he seemed to mistake my silence for chastisement. "What? I like movies."

The drive back through town seems to take one-tenth of the time that the outbound journey had consumed. Darkness has fallen completely by the time that we pull into my driveway, and after quickly walking Mercury, we settle into the couch for a movie or twelve. He immediately snuggles into my chest, my arm draped around him. His head is arranged in such a manner that the top of his Mohawk would tickle my nose from time to time.

I do not mind it at all.

After the first movie, I open a bottle of wine and pour us each a glass. Having always preferred reds, I automatically choose a pinot noir in the event he has not yet developed a taste for the drier varietals. I hand him a glass, suggest that we step outside to smoke, and have made it almost to the back porch when I realize he is not following me. I turn and see him looking in his glass, puzzled.

"I haven't had a lot of wine," he says, uncertainly.

"Is that a good thing or a bad thing?" I ask.

"Does it taste good?"

"Try it and find out."

He holds the glass up to his lips, pausing at the last minute, his nose inside the perimeter of the rim, and inhales deeply. Satisfied, he tips the glass up just enough to let a few drops of the ruby liquid slip into his mouth, holding it there for a few seconds before swallowing. He winces slightly, the telltale sign of a person who is not accustomed to the tannins found in red wines.

"It's, it's…" Suddenly, I am in panic mode, mentally running through my inventory, hoping I had another option. Didn't I pick up a white the other day?

"It's good. No one has ever given me any before," he says. "At least, nothing this good."

Good? He likes it? My heart leaps, not because he likes the same kind of wine that I enjoy, but because I am able to watch him try something new, something he might not have considered before. Innocence is not the total domain of children; we all carry some level of innocence with us throughout our entire lives. We may never recognize it again after adolescence, but we have it with us nonetheless. The pure joy at bearing witness to this innocence breaking through the hardened shell of experience is a miracle to behold.

The fact that Prince Charming looks extremely cute during the process is just a bonus.

We settle onto the back porch—me in a chair right outside the door, him on the torn linoleum that covers the back steps. We talk of everything and nothing, sipping the pinot noir and smoking. He tells me about his past, his secrets, his baggage, and I find myself telling him mine. We compare notes, and realize that while we had not moved in the same circles, we do know several of the same people.

"So it's like a Venn diagram," I start, but stop short at the look in his eyes. He almost looks... hurt. "What's wrong?"

"I don't know what that is..." His voice falters at the end, like he is ashamed. "I'm not smart."

"Bullshit."

"No, seriously..." He is starting to crumble. I know I need to act fast, but I do not know what to do. Closing my eyes, I consider several options, but in the end, simply say the first thing that pops into my mind.

"You know what Confucius say?" I ask, barely able to suppress my grin.

"What?" he huffs.

"Man who stand on toilet is high on pot."

My eyes still closed, I can feel the silence in the air, until with a single sound it is shattered. The tension vanishes instantly as he starts to laugh, first quietly, then snowballing into a raucous expression of pure joy.

I can only assume I have chosen the right thing to say.

Eventually the laughter subsides, and he smiles at me; pure happiness radiates out of his indigo blue eyes.

"God, I haven't laughed like that in ages," he says, his eyes never leaving mine.

"Me either. I really don't emote very... well. It's never really been my strong suit." I am shocked with the ease at which I can tell him even my most well-guarded vulnerabilities.

I notice our glasses were empty, and pluck them from the cement floor of the porch.

"No more for me. If I'm laughing, I'm obviously already getting drunk," he says, though he seemed far from intoxicated.

"Seriously?"

"No. I'm not even tipsy. I just want to keep my head clear," he says, a smirk turning up one corner of his lips. "I want to remember this."

"Well, if you wanted to laugh," I say, steering clear of his last statement, "you came to the right house. My first name means 'laughter', after all."

"Good to know."

I start back into the house with our glasses, Prince Charming standing up, stretching his long arms over his head. I can just make out the top of a tattoo on his lower back, but do not give it much thought.

"What does your name mean?" I ask, over my shoulder.

"Gift of God," he said simply.

I stop dead in my tracks, and the next sound I hear is the explosion of two wine glasses as they shatter on the concrete.

We wind up turning the three-day weekend in to four, and we spend the time doing… everything. We argue about the characters in *Star Wars*, and discuss computers at a level of detail that I normally only find at work. I cook for him and he takes me out to dinner. I even take him over to a friend's house for fondue and mint juleps, anxious to show off my new…

It suddenly strikes me that I did not know what to call him. Friend? Boyfriend?

Soul mate.

Alongside that realization comes another. Weeks before, with True Love's Kiss, Prince Charming had begun the process of waking me from my three-and-a-half-decade slumber. And here, now, in this moment, my eyes are finally wide open, quite possibly for the very first time in my life.

I never want to go back to sleep again.

I have found my soul's true mate. And while there is neither a bolt of lightning, nor a clap of thunder, nor scales falling from my eyes, the transformation in me is equally extreme in its completeness. Magic has entered my life, and while my logic never truly disappears, it works with my emotions to create a newer, better, more complete set of beings that will be, and perhaps had always been, intertwined for eternity.

That following Friday, I play hooky from work, slipping out of bed just long enough to grab my laptop. As I ease myself back under the covers, Prince Charming grunts in his sleep, twists the sheet in his hands, and rolls away from me. From where I sit with my back against the headboard, I can see that he is completely exposed, and I finally get a really good look at that tattoo on his lower back. It is an ancient Egyptian pictograph: the Eye of Horus, the protector. Memories slam together in my mind, and I can almost hear Artemis' tinkling laughter in my head.

In reality, all I hear are the bells of St. John's Episcopal Church, around the corner, chiming the noon hour.

The
Seven Dwarves

I AM STILL THIRTY-SIX YEARS OLD, but now I have seven men on my mind.

I am neither hopelessly dwelling on my past, nor am I standing on a corner in Winslow, Arizona—although—to this day, two would like to stone me, four might want to get back together with me, and only one I consider my friend. In fact, I am standing on my cousin's back porch in Reston, Virginia, a cigarette between two fingers, as Prince Charming slumbers upstairs. I am too excited to sleep, and for a very good reason.

Today is my wedding day.

It is the middle of September, and even the weather itself seems to be celebrating our union. The sky is free of clouds, but without glare or an overabundance of brightness. It is warm, yet still cool enough to warrant a long-sleeved shirt due to the breeze that slips through the perfectly-spaced, upright slits in the privacy fence around the tiny backyard. While my cousin's townhouse feels somewhat secluded, I can still hear the ambient sounds of any urban area – automobile engines, horns, airplanes, and even the dull hum of electricity as it runs through the wires. These are sounds that all who have dwelt in a city have learned to relegate into the background, mostly without a conscious thought.

In less than twelve hours, I will exchange rings and vows with Prince Charming within the confines of the District of Columbia. When everything is said and done, we will be legally married, at least within the District and the handful of states which will recognize our union. Would that our home state of Georgia were among that number, but it is not.

This is but one of the many downfalls of living in a liberal city located within the borders of a conservative state.

Considering my proximity to my destination, it seems only natural that my thoughts should turn to the path that brought me to today. While there were actually nine who came before Prince Charming, only seven were of any import. Those seven, however magnificent in their own ways, can never compare to the flawed perfection that is the embodiment and the essence of the man to whom I chose to be wed. In the metaphorical sense (and in six of their cases, the physical sense), Prince Charming towers over his predecessors, reducing them not only in stature, but also in memory, to the size of a dwarf.

If any of the Dwarves could come close to Prince Charming in physical stature, it was the first—Bashful. Both have blue eyes, but it is there that their physical distinction ended. Where Prince Charming is slender and willowy, Bashful had been carved in the style of the Nordic gods of old.

Introduced through mutual friends, we quickly decided to pursue each other, despite the fact that I was not only still on active duty in the Navy, but I lived more than four hundred miles away from his mountain home.

It was late spring, and I resolved to surprise Bashful by making the trip but not telling him. I stopped occasionally at pay phones to make sure he was home, but otherwise, he thought I was safely ensconced in the base housing unit, whiling away the hours. I even stopped a few miles away from his house and changed into my dress whites, wanting to fulfill an oft-mentioned fantasy of his—the sailor returned from sea.

I will never forget the look in his eyes when he opened the door and saw me, sea bag on my shoulder, "dog dish" sailor's cap cocked to the side of my head.

"Oh, shit."

Oh… what?

He recovered quickly, and soon swept me up into his arms, pulling me into his house, showering me with affection. It was after an hour of "catching up" that he finally explained his initial exclamation.

"I'm supposed to have dinner with my parents tonight," he said. "My grandmother's there and she's making all my favorites."

Instantly forgiving him, I said I was tired and wanted to rest a bit—I had hoped we would head out to the clubs that evening, and even in the short time I had been a member of the "scene," I had learned the importance of a "disco nap."

"Would you like to come with me?"

The question hung in the air, its importance self-evident. He wanted to introduce me to his family.

"Um..." I eloquently answered, my conversational skill suddenly plummeting. "Do they know that you're..."

"Gay?"

"Um, yeah."

"Yes. I told them about a year ago, right before I moved here," he said, his eyes growing distant.

"Well," I stalled. This was an important undertaking.

I was about to meet his parents.

What would I do if the situation were reversed, and I had just asked someone to come home and meet my family? I dismissed the thought almost as soon as it had surfaced. At that time I thought I would never invite someone home to meet my family again. During college, I had asked my girlfriend to join us for Sunday dinner after attending church once, and my mother was cold, snarky and referred to her as "Mrs. Robinson" the entire day. It would be years before I would see The Graduate and understand the reference, although to be fair, she and I were a lot closer in age—eighteen and thirty—than Dustin Hoffman and Anne Bancroft were.

"Yes," I heard myself answer. "I'll go."

"Let me give them a call to make sure there's enough food."

Growing up in the South, one learns quickly this is a call that is always made, but never required. It is a smoke-screen used to advise a host of additional guests, potential awkwardness, or, in the more extreme cases, a necessity for legal representation. There is always enough food; Southerners do not know how to cook any other way.

He made the call while I changed out of my uniform. While Clinton's "Don't Ask, Don't Tell" policy had been passed a year before, I did not want to tempt fate.

That evening, I met Bashful's Mother and Father, and a short whirlwind of a woman who only seemed to answer to "Nana," although I doubt that was her given name. The table groaned underneath the weight of the seemingly dozens of dishes she had prepared for dinner with her favorite grandson.

"Mom, Dad, Nana," Bashful began, but his upper teeth trapped his lower lip and he stopped speaking. He looked at me, and I could see... something in his eyes. I could not identify the emotion, but it almost seemed like... fear?

"This is my friend," he said.

While I'm sure he said my name afterwards, I stopped listening at "friend."

His friend? I could not believe what I was hearing. This was a man who had plucked up the courage to tell his parents something which, during the early to mid-1990's, was still a hard conversation to have. The AIDS crisis of the 1980's was still very fresh in everyone's mind, as were the more-frequent-than-not news reports of homosexuals under attack at military bases, colleges, universities, and high schools. He managed to hold down a job, go to school, and despite my own, personal visual verification that he did, in fact, have "a pair," he called me his...

Friend.

Well, of course, I was his friend, but he had told me I was so much more than simply a friend. He told me that every day, when he called me his boyfriend, his lover, but to his family, I was just his...

Friend.

I suddenly realized why the look he gave me before making the introduction was so familiar; I had seen it often enough in the eyes of my own father: shame.

Bashful was ashamed of me. I scarcely remember anything else from that night, much less the entire weekend. While it had begun with the best of intentions, it had ended in fear and disappointment. I returned to my seaside home in Virginia, and never saw Bashful, a Dwarf trapped in the body of a Nordic god, again.

I hear the heavy footfalls of Prince Charming as he stumbles across the hallway to the bathroom, grateful that my cousin and her husband are already at work, for Prince Charming is not at his perceptive best immediately after waking.

In addition, he has a preference for minimal sleepwear, if he chooses to wear any at all.

I turn to head inside, suddenly wanting of his usual bleary-eyed early-morning affection. As I move inside and slide the glass door closed behind me, I give Bashful one last, departing thought.

Despite their physical similarities, Bashful and Prince Charming could not be more different. While Prince Charming is neither devoid of modesty nor restraint, one could easily make that assumption based on his behavior. He called his parents before the sun had set on that fateful Memorial Day three and a half months ago, and not only told them about me, but about how he felt about me, and the impact I was making in his life. Within another week, he had invited them to our home for lunch, and before they departed for their three-hour drive home, I had already begun to form a small connection with both his mother and his father. As far as they were concerned, my inclusion into their family was a foregone conclusion.

While I have rarely borne witness to such passion and enthusiasm in my life, I never dreamed that I would be the subject of such excitement.

I was half-tempted to figure out how to say "Go Big, or Go Home" in Latin if for no other reason than to have it made into our new family crest.

After Bashful came Sneezy, a more locally-sourced companion, who did not, in fact, receive his appellation due to the size of his nose.

Instead, he seemed to constantly suffer from seasonal allergies.

Sneezy and I were both on active duty in Norfolk, he on the *USS Enterprise* while I still languished in the Transient Personnel Unit. I would tell everyone later that I only went out with him because of his duty station. Having watched *Star Trek* with my father since childhood, to be that close to a ship named the Enterprise was enough to warrant dinner and a movie.

Before long, we were both drummed out of the service, and I had a two-bedroom townhouse walking distance from one of the smaller, local beaches. Sneezy loved to spend his time there, and it was a popular hangout for the small gay population in the area. He would be gone for hours on end, but would always come home in the evening seeming relaxed and calm.

Sneezy and I acted our ages—we made bad decisions, chose substances over substance, and in general, squandered our youth rather than acting like responsible adults. This more than anything was what led to our complete lack of money, an pending eviction, and virtually unemployable.

The temporary work we were able to find was sporadic, so Sneezy offered a solution, one which shocked me: we could move in with his parents.

In stark contrast to his predecessor (who had relegated me to simply being his friend), Sneezy not only told his forebears exactly who I was, but wanted to share their home with me.

I was shocked when they agreed, saving me from returning to my home in Atlanta in disgrace, having been kicked out of the Navy rather than excelling at it. We packed all our meager belongings into a rented truck, and drove all night to the small, smelly town in Wisconsin, the local aroma courtesy of a paper mill just on the outskirts of the city limits.

Perhaps, had we made this move in any other month than January, I might have enjoyed my time there; however, my life as a Midwesterner was not meant to be.

Three months after our early-morning arrival, Sneezy walked into the room that we shared and asked if we could talk.

For the record, if you want to scare me to death, simply say this phrase: "We need to talk." In addition to the adrenal response, my brain will quickly run through every single permutation of how the conversation will go, select the most outlandish and remote possibility, and then focus on that choice until I'm physically sick with worry.

It is an unfortunate coincidence that those remote outliers almost always turn out to be exactly what happens.

While back in his hometown, Sneezy had rekindled a couple of friendships from high school, which led to introductions to members of the local community. While I was busy doing things like looking for a job, and trying to make us self-sufficient, Sneezy was having sex with one of these people. His new partner of choice was the local purveyor of marijuana, and while I had never understood the attraction to the psychoactive smoke produced by the dried green, crumpled flower buds, I did not judge.

Sneezy and the Other One continued to court each other, first physically, then emotionally. They even traveled out of town overnight together in order to view some feat of engineering on the other side of the state. I can still recall the amount of passion with which Sneezy possessed me upon his return, thinking it odd as he had never been so physically forthcoming with me.

What I did not know at the time was that the Other One, during their trip, had confessed that his physical attraction had grown beyond its own boundaries, and that he was in love with my boyfriend.

It was up to Sneezy to decide, and soon I found myself riding a Greyhound bus from one side of the country to the other, my mother's instructions on self-reflection ignored, choosing instead to reflect upon that which I had lost, rather than that which I had to gain.

By the time we pulled into a stop in Cincinnati, I had convinced myself that the last lovemaking session, the one where he surprised me with the amount of passion he showed, was my audition, and I had failed. He would rather be with a high-school dropout drug dealer than be with me.

I am again grateful that my cousin and her husband are at work, because while it would have been a bit awkward for Prince Charming and I to shower together with them at home, we would have done it anyway. We are both very clean as we go to dress for our big day.

We prepare for the ceremony which was now less than four hours away. While neither of us are remotely virginal, I still choose to wear white. The choice to elope is the best decision we could have made. It frees us from family entanglements, and allows us to wear dress shirts and jeans to the wedding. He wears a black button-up in contrast to my white one, though both with a similar damask pattern over the left shoulder. Finally ready, we take a cab into DC proper.

My cousin does not drink coffee, and therefore her home is devoid of any. However, Prince Charming and I consume enough of the bitter brew to ensure that the nation of Columbia remains solvent for years to come. We locate a Starbucks close to the White House and sit outside, enjoying not only the weather, but our last few hours as "single" men. I take a sip of my peppermint mocha latte, and am once more transported into the past, neither to Bashful nor Sneezy, but to the one who came had actually introduced me to this particular combination of flavors. He was the third man to whom I would offer my heart: Grumpy.

It had been several years since Sneezy had sent me home in shame, and I had already been transformed by Artemis into something resembling a socially-unawkward being. Hestia and I had already met, and I had even made friends with the cast of the cabaret show at Backstreet, spending my weekends helping out backstage. It was one night at the cabaret when I met Grumpy, standing in line for the bathroom. We met, and he smiled. We talked, and exchanged numbers.

I called him, and this apparently was cause for a great amount of surprise on his part. During this phone conversation, I apparently said all the right things, as he later confided in me that he swooned.

I was quite sure I had never made anyone swoon before. As with Sneezy before him, we were soon living together, but before that could happen, I had to understand one thing:

Grumpy liked marijuana. In fact, Grumpy liked marijuana so much, that he was able to convince me to try some with him. Soon, I joined him daily in the fuzzy enhancement that comes accompanies cannabis.

Grumpy also liked himself, though he would ensure that he appeared humble to the outside world. During the half-decade that we were together—a new personal record, mind you—he was always telling anyone who would listen how horrible things were, and how the dysfunctional status of our lives were all my fault.

I offered no argument, but instead allowed my mind to wander freely. That is, after all, what one does when stoned for five and a half years.

In the early stages of our relationship, I faced fierce competition for Grumpy's affection. One particularly harrowing holiday season, we were exchanging gifts and I instinctively reached for the last present under the tree—a beautiful box, much more extravagantly wrapped than the ones I had just torn through.

"That's not for you," he said softly.

"Oh, sorry." I was embarrassed. "Who's it for?"

"Someone else, silly. Pass me the pipe?"

Quickly, both the room and our minds were clouded.

The present was for another gentleman caller. After weeks of casual courting, said caller had invited Grumpy to a mountain cabin to ring in the new year.

Grumpy accepted the invitation, leaving me in our shared home, alone for the holiday.

He returned, several days later, but shockingly without his new beau in tow. I never discovered why they did not work out; I really did not care.

"What do we do now?" I asked, unsure of what was happening.

"Do you want to get back together?" he asked, the snark evident in his voice.

"I believe I do," I answered, shocked at my own response.

"Then woo me," he said. "I don't think you can pull it off."

Anyone who has spent more than an hour in my company can attest that one of the best ways to get me to do anything, whether I like it or not, is to simply imply that it is beyond my capabilities.

As one of my best friends would later put it, I would hear "I triple-dog-dare you" in every challenge, whether it was said or not.

Grumpy was from up north, and while this, at the time, would normally disqualify him from any romantic entanglement with me, I had made an exception. After about three years together, his whole family had driven down for a visit. They all went to dinner, however, an invitation was not extended to me. I knew that things were tense between Grumpy and his parents, mostly owing to his sexuality.

I honestly did not care whether or not I went out to dinner with them; instead I enjoyed the time I spent at home, with Mary Jane and our six cats.

We had not yet become cellular phone owners, so there was no warning when he bolted into our apartment.

"I need you to go to your office," he said, out of breath from hefting his growing weight up the two flights of stairs that led to our third-story apartment. "My parents want to see the place."

"Well, invite them in, silly," I said, not quite grasping the situation.

"I need you to go to your office," he repeated. We had converted the second bedroom of our apartment into an office which allowed me to work from home on some days, and gave me an escape on others.

The full weight of what he was asking dawned on me, and his careful phrasing served only one purpose: it allowed him to ask me to hide myself without actually, word-for-word, asking me to do it.

I'm glad he was able to bring himself that comfort. After all, life with me was horrible. I mean, just ask anyone to whom he spoke.

Out of shock more than anything else, I stood and staggered into my office, and he pulled the door shut behind me. I heard his family's voices as he showed them around our home, and proudly indicated precious possessions that we had acquired. It could have been for five minutes, or it could have been five hours. I heard them leave, but instead of escaping my prison, I opened the blinds, and watched his family walk through the courtyard back to their car.

I wanted to see what kind of people would ask to see their son's home, but insist that his partner be hidden away first. Apparently, they were Yankees.

I heard the door to my office open behind me, but my sanctuary was lost forever, my refuge now turned into yet another Tower. Grumpy had done the exact same thing that Bashful had done, but in spades.

Not long after that incident, we decided to separate, staying together but living apart, and shortly after that, he suggested that we spend an entire month apart, with absolutely no contact, perhaps to see if distance truly does make the heart grow fonder.

Once again, I was being asked to audition for someone's affection, and once again I failed. Three days before the separation period was to be over—a date I had highlighted in yellow on my calendar—he called, and asked if we could speak that night. Knowing that I could not wait any longer than I already had, he told me over the phone that we were to be no more.

The same crushing devastation visited upon me by Sneezy had returned, but it did not last as long. Soon, I was back on my feet, growing, learning, and, shockingly, thriving.

It would be nearly seven years before I learned the truth about why he had jumped the gun instead of letting the month run out.

One of my closest friends, known to me as Hestia, had gotten wind of the situation and found it at odds with her virtues as protector of the home and the hearth. Unbeknownst to anyone other than herself, she drove three hours from her home in South Carolina to Atlanta, where, after relentlessly pounding on his door, she took Grumpy to a park for a chat.

By "chat," she meant lecture. She informed him that stringing me along was cruel, and that he had better make a decision, make it fast, or face physical harm. He returned to his apartment, she to her home, and the next day I received the call.

Until she revealed her involvement herself nearly a decade later, I never realized Hestia had seen the situation for what it was, and rather than face my predictable denials and rebuffs, she went straight to the source and fixed the problem.

I'm glad my girlfriends have always been goddesses.

The time for our nuptials is nearly upon us, and we enter the blockish courthouse on Indiana Avenue. After checking with the reception desk, we ride escalators up to the fourth floor, where inside the Marriage Bureau, two of our guests have already arrived.

Cora is one of my colleagues from work, and she and her long-time beau Todd have made the trip down from Harrisburg to bear witness to our ceremony.

Personally, I think my boss sent her just to ensure that the wedding was actually happening.

My cousin and her husband are running a tad late, but we are assured that, as long as they arrive in the next half hour, we will still be on schedule.

We relax in chairs that are standard for this type of building, my hand on Prince Charming's knee, and his arm around my shoulders. We converse with Cora and Todd about various mundane things: at which restaurant would we to eat for our post-wedding lunch (for which they had already insisted on paying), what are our plans while we're still in the District, how long will we be in town, *et cetera, et cetera, et cetera.*

"For two people about to tie the knot, you don't look nervous at all," observes Cora.

"Should we be nervous?" I ask, concerned that, once again, I've taken a fatal misstep.

"We're doing what we're supposed to be doing," said Prince Charming softly. Despite his normal, over-the-top manner, he can be shy at times, especially in unfamiliar situations or with new acquaintances.

It is absolutely adorable.

"He's right, you know," I agree, my voice speaking, but the words coming from somewhere else. "I knew the second I saw him that I wanted to spend the rest of my life with him."

Cora smiles, and begins to speak, but we are interrupted by a flurry of action at the door as my cousin and her husband make their arrival. Todd jumps up to alert the staff that we are now ready, and before I know what is happening, I am standing with Prince Charming beneath an awning decorated with silk flowers in all manner of spring colors, a petite woman standing between us.

Great. Now I *am* nervous, and I am looking at my shoes.

As the officiant reads the traditional opening phrases of the wedding ceremony from a small, white booklet that she holds in front of her, Prince Charming reaches forward and gently presses upward on my chin, bringing my gaze once more into his magnificent, sapphire eyes.

We promise to love, comfort, and honor each other. We vow to keep each other and forsake all others for the rest of our lives. We each place a ring on the other's hands, his ring first, then my ring.

As I hear him speak of richer and poorer, better and worse, sickness and health, he begins to struggle with my ring, and fears of old once again begin to make their assault.

Is this a sign that it is not meant to be?

As soon as the idea enters my head, it was gone. The ring slips over my knuckle, swollen from years of cracking, and nestles securely against the breadth of my hand, where it fits my finger perfectly.

The fears are instantly replaced with comfort, and with the knowledge that the struggle was not to prevent the giving of the ring, but, now given, to ensure that it be nearly impossible to remove.

The petite woman whose name I have long since forgotten pronounces us legally married, and before she can ask if we would like to seal our union with a kiss, Prince Charming has my face in his hands, and is pulling me toward him. I tilt my head, to allow him easier access to that which, not because of the ceremony we are performing, but because of a three-day weekend that had turned into four earlier that year, is completely, totally, and wholly his.

Our lips touch, and the entire room vanishes. We are standing in a hallway, stretching infinitely in both directions. To one side, I see images of the past—a couple in Victorian England, resplendent in what we now call "period" dress. Behind them are two pageboys in the service of some medieval lord, and behind them, swathed in togas, are two men locked in heated but companionable discourse; no animosity exists between them. At the edge of my vision, I can see one last couple, dusky-skinned, with plaited hair, one wearing the uniform of an Egyptian soldier, the other in the scholarly dress that I can only assume was worn by those who might have curated the Great Library of Alexandria. The hallway continues even further beyond these two, though any other occupants are lost in the distance.

To the other side, I can also see couples, but their forms are less distinct. Fate has not chosen what shapes will be occupied by the two immortal souls who, after years of searching, finally found each other.

I will never know if Prince Charming also saw eternity laid bare as we kissed that day, under the arch, in Washington, DC, but in my quietest moments, when my fears threaten to overwhelm me, I can still retreat to that hallway, where the past watches with kindness, and the future is yet to be decided.

After Grumpy, I had no desire for any lingering commitment, and found myself in a slow decline toward confirmed bachelorhood.

Happy and I met on Valentine's Day, and while we were never really suited for each other romantically, we were quite platonically compatible. We would remain friends for years, meeting up for the occasional night out from time to time.

After Happy came Doc, who I met, not through mutual friends, or through the now-prevalent Internet, but as the Good Lord intended: blind drunk at a bar. He was an architect, and was able to engage my brain on a level which his predecessors could never have attained. Unfortunately, the circumstances of our first meeting colored the remainder of our three-month fling, each encounter saturated with enough ethanol to send an entire Alabama county to Alcoholics Anonymous.

A few years after Doc there was Sleepy, and quite frankly, it seemed that was pretty much all we did. We worked opposite schedules—he worked nine-to-five, while I was a night owl still trapped in the hospitality industry. Within a month of that relationship beginning it was over. There is, after all, only so much fun can have with someone when you're both unconscious.

Dopey was the last of the Dwarves, my final attempt at an actual "relationship." We began with earnest enough intentions, however, my work schedule required me to be out of town on weekdays, and only allowed for two days at home before heading back out on the road. The only thing I remember about Dopey is that we would have broken up a lot sooner if I had been in town more often.

The guy was a complete idiot.

Shortly after Dopey and I called it quits, I met up with Happy at the Ansley Square shopping center in Midtown, where not one, but four bars were clustered around a sloped parking lot. We were at Burkhart's, or Felix's, or Oscar's (as we frequently would make stops in at least three out of the four) when he asked me the strangest question:

"Who is your perfect guy?"

"I've told you, dear," I replied. "I don't have a type."

"You might not have a type, but you have a perfect guy. We all do. We just never seem to find them."

Happy was four years older than me, though for some reason he always managed to look ten years younger. Like me, he too seemed resigned to the fact that not everyone finds their soul's true mate.

"But, seriously," he pressed the point. "If you could build the perfect guy, what would he look like?"

I stare at the oversized, classically triangular glass in front of me, my mind beginning to wander a bit more freely. Either due to the olive-free martinis or in spite of them, I found myself giving the question some serious thought. My eyes began to lose focus, the noise in the bar seemed to become a touch more muted, and the lights seemed to dim ever so slightly. Happy and I were drawn into our own little world, the rest of the real world moving along around us.

"Taller than me," I said, suddenly. While I could never be described as overly tall, at six-feet-flat, I found myself at least half-a-head, if not a whole one, taller than anyone I met. I had recently developed a new appreciation for some of Artemis' dating difficulties, though to be fair, I found gay men were much less sensitive on the subject than their heterosexual counterparts. Bashful suddenly leapt into my mind, and I remembered one of his physical characteristics that I found most enticing. "I want to be able to rest my head on someone's shoulder."

"Why?" asked Happy.

"Easy," I answered, before I took another sip, more as a stalling tactic than a desire to become further intoxicated, though the latter did not hurt. "Because, when held, it makes me feel safe."

In vino veritas.

"I assume 'pretty' is a foregone conclusion," said Happy, but I cut him off.

"Nope, 'pretty' isn't even on the list." On this point I am quite firm. "That word means different things to different people. As does 'stunning', 'handsome', and my personal favorite, 'breath-taking'."

"I want someone to take my breath away; whether or not he is perceived in the same manner by others really does not interest me in the least."

I spared Happy a quick glance, saw him writing something on a cocktail napkin, and assumed it was his phone number. Honestly, at the rate he gives it out, he should just have business cards printed.

"Blue eyes," I continued. "I've always loved blue eyes. Blond hair wouldn't hurt either, but neither are really requirements. Slender is better," I paused for dramatic effect "but again, not a requirement. I don't know, this all seems a bit silly."

"Why?"

"Because all of this is negotiable," I responded, my mind entering a sort-of fugue state, where the thoughts become words without benefit of a social filter. "There is no mathematical formula that can show me who I should spend my life with. There's no algorithm that can predict, with any acceptable amount of accuracy, my Mister Right. Trust me, I've looked."

Happy was still writing on the napkin; maybe the intended recipient must be getting his e-mail address, home address, and breakfast order as well.

"We could sit here all night, and I could make a list that basically says I want a former porn star in his mid-twenties with blond hair, blue eyes, who is at least six-one and has an ass off which I could bounce a roll of quarters. I could say he doesn't have to be smarter than me, but has to at least be able to engage with me. And, just for good measure, let's add in a love of science fiction and fantasy that borders on obsession.

"Let's see," I continued, "that barely covers physical, and just scratches the surface of intellectual. What about emotional? He should have flaws, but the flaws must be compatible with my own."

Happy suddenly stopped writing, perhaps realizing that our conversation had gone from light-hearted and playful to deep and existential in one martini flat. I ordered another round.

"Did you just actually admit you have flaws?" he asked, the false amazement in his voice apparent.

"Shut up," I said. "You asked the question."

"I know, I know," he said returning to his writing. The bartender brought our drinks, and rather than wait for it to be placed before me, I reached out and seized it directly out of his hand. Our fingers brushed, but there was no electricity in the connection; there hasn't been electricity in any connection for quite some time. I begin to wonder if my dalliances with the Dwarves, especially toward the end, were performed more out of duty than desire.

"Yes, I would prefer someone younger than me, if for no other reason than my 'he-must-be-at-least-thirty' rule hasn't exactly worked out all that well. I don't really care as much about the age difference as I do the fact that I want him to be able to show me a different perspective on things. He needs to be old enough to have had a past, to have some experiences behind him. He needs to be a genuinely nice guy, but have a bad-boy exterior. I want him to be able to do the things I can't, the things that I'm afraid to do myself. I want someone who can engage me on all levels—physical, romantic, spiritual, sexual, emotional, intellectual, and... and..."

My fugue was over, and the momentum was gone. I turned and looked at Happy, only to find him staring at me, wide-eyed, his mouth open slightly, his expression one of shock. He realized I was looking, and shook off his daze. The ambient sounds and lights of the bar begin to return to their full saturation, and Happy folds up the cocktail napkin on which he had been writing. What he does next baffles me.

"Here you go, darling," he says, either his Tuscaloosa drawl or his level of intoxication lengthening the vowels. "Don't lose it"

"Sweetie," I said, perplexed. "I already have your number."

"Read it."

I opened the napkin and read what Happy had written. Even in the subdued light of the bar I could make out most of the words, written in his messy scrawl: "young(er)," "blond," "blue eyes," "tall," "flawed," "smart," "nerdy." The list continued, summarizing everything about which I had been speaking.

I looked up at my friend, still confused, but oddly grateful, though I did not know why.

"What am I supposed to do with this?" I asked, waving the napkin half-heartedly with one hand.

"Keep it," he said. "Someone did it to me a couple of weeks ago, and it's really helped."

"How?" I am still stunned at Happy's sudden depth of character; he is not normally so perceptive this late in the evening.

"Because," he said, setting his credit card on the bar, signaling the end of our time here. "How can you know if you've found the right person if you don't know what you're looking for?"

As I looked over the list, the logical part of my brain quickly noted that to find all the traits I had described would be astronomically improbable. It was then that I began to wonder if I should just give up on love altogether, but my inner soul-searching stopped short when I saw what Happy had written at the very bottom of the napkin:

"Amazing ass."

I spent the next five minutes trying to figure out if I could actually strangle Happy get away with it.

Following our wedding and a kiss that threatens to bump the nervous-looking couple in the lobby into the next time slot, we walk a couple of blocks where Cora and Todd treat all of us to lunch. The National Archives are nearby, and Prince Charming and I have recently begun what would turn into a multi-year discussion of the Constitution and its impact on our government. My cousin and her husband return to work, and Cora, Todd, along with myself and Prince Charming stroll several blocks to view the original document itself. Afterward, our wedding guests say their goodbyes, as they have plans with friends this evening and need to get to the other side of town.

We take the Metro over to where the White House sits overlooking at the National Mall, and amble the few, short blocks to the Capitol Hilton, where I have reserved a room. All my travel during the Days of Dopey have paid off. Due to my elite status with the hotel chain, we are upgraded to a suite instantly, and to be honest, it feels good to have my new husband's eyes widen in amazement as the front desk staff bends over backwards to accommodate us.

I even feel a little bit sexy.

As we ride the elevator to the top floor, I attempt restraint, and I make it a full three seconds before I slam Prince Charming into the side of the car with a kiss that is, while romantic, meant to convey another, more basic human desire.

Sunlight streams through the windows that run the length of the suite, filtering through sheer fabric that offers only the most minimal modicum of modesty. We are both exhausted and energized by the day's events, and soon are stretched out on the king-sized bed, our bodies intertwined, our heads touching.

The day is simultaneously exactly like every day that has preceded it, yet completely and totally different. I have only recently begun to realize the sense of duality that is inherent not only nature, but seems to be at the core of the universe itself. The vision of eternal destiny that I saw during our first kiss as a married couple is still echoing in my mind, and it will do so for the rest of my life. We have not discussed what I saw, but we both seem to be operating under its influence. As he kisses me, his lungs pull the air from mine, as my lungs pull the air from his.

To completely share someone's heart, soul, mind or body are both amazing pleasures and tremendous honors. To be bestowed all four at once is a blessing on a scale that can only be described as cosmic.

Prince Charming drags his finger across my chest, the gentle pressure on the starched shirt sending electric shocks throughout my whole body.

"What are you doing?" I ask, breathless.

"Writing my name. You're mine, now. You're stuck with me forever."

"I know," I laugh. "I was at the wedding, too, you know."

"That's not what I mean, silly," he responds, then pulls away from the embrace and rolls onto his back, his eyes fixed on the ceiling.

I can see a multitude of emotions in his eyes, each one fighting for superiority over the other, none of them winning.

"Why did you say yes?" he asks, holding up his left hand and staring at the ring.

"Why did you ask?" I respond, staring at his profile. He turns his head and our eyes meet.

"Because I wanted to," he says.

"And there you have your answer."

I am rewarded with what I have come to call the Pure Smile. It is not grandiose or over-the-top, but subtle, gentle, curving of the lips beneath eyes that seem to radiate light.

"Go start the shower, I'll be there in a minute," I say, ordering my Prince away, but only for the merest of moments. He stands and pulls his shirt off over his head as he walks toward the other end of the suite. I watch him walk away, the Eye of Horus tattoo inked across the small of his back, casting its watchful gaze at me, and am suddenly aware that Prince Charming is now my protector, my caretaker.

I always tell people that his rear end is so perfectly shaped that I do not mind watching him walk away from me. That, in all honesty, is only partially true. The other reason I do not mind watching him walk away is that I know he will always return.

I awkwardly climb to my feet and follow my... *husband.* The cherished word is both easy to accept and hard to believe, as is the weight that has been added to my left hand, courtesy of a titanium band, inlaid with blue cobalt.

I wonder if he ever realized that I suggested these particular rings because the color of the inlay reminds me of the color of his eyes the night we first met.

I join him in the bathroom, the steam from the near-scalding water already coating the mirror. I wipe away some of the condensation with a white washcloth, and look at myself.

I could use a shower myself. After all, I've got a big night ahead of me.

As I unbutton my shirt and hang it on the back of the door so the wrinkles will loosen in the steam-filled room, I am suddenly struck by the irony of the situation.

We are going to celebrate our wedding night—at least the first part of it—simply by going out to dinner, and then seeing a movie for which I had purchased tickets three weeks ago. These are activities which couples usually choose in the early days of courting, not immediately after tying the knot. Yet, the more I think about it, the more it makes sense.

We never really had a "traditional" first date, choosing to eschew the awkward courting phase and give ourselves over to what the Fates had planned. Now we are newlyweds on our honeymoon, and dinner and a movie sounds like the perfect way to start our marriage.

 Cloudy with a Chance of Grimm

I am thirty-eight years old, and I am happy.

I move through the rooms of our home, voices from the past and present moving with me. A long-desired, yet still hastily planned party is underway, and there are just enough people to make our house feel full, but not crowded. Although counterintuitive to the long-ago and forcibly-indoctrinated training as a proper host, I really want nothing more than to politely thank everyone for coming, and promptly toss them out the front door, their coats and handbags to follow.

Prince Charming is wearing very tight jeans, every contour of his body in denim bas relief, leaving nothing to the imagination. I have been fighting the urge to pull him aside and ravish him in the coat closet, yet thus far have managed something resembling restraint. I turn back to my duties as host, and begin an irregular route through the difference spaces, ensuring that wine glasses are full, and that empty plates have been cleared.

Our home is not large; it is not new. The floor in my study needs to be replaced, and there are dings in the paint everywhere. After more than three years of occupancy, we have only managed to paint and decorate a single room, and only a hallway at that.

Seven feet long and three feet wide, the hallway serves as a junction between five rooms—five archways cut from the field of the walls, leaving very little surface area with which to work. These walls have now been painted a deep, velvety chocolate brown, but hardly any of the color can be seen.

With such an awkwardly shaped space, made worse by the curious placement of the electrical fuse box, we were at a loss as far as decor was concerned, until I remembered a recent trip to Chicago where a colleague and dear friend took me to dinner at the Next Door Bistro, a lively, crowded place featuring exquisite Italian-American fare. Whether traditional or stereotypical, the bistro walls were covered in black-and-white photographs of previous diners, some well-known to me, while some were, I assumed, local celebrities.

Inspiration struck.

During that momentous Memorial Day weekend nearly three years prior, Prince Charming and I had fallen in love for many reasons: fate, desire and passion were only a few. Another of those reasons was our mutual love of movies and television.

Due to some cosmic coincidence, we both possessed the ability to completely immerse ourselves in the entertainment provided, allowing our emotions to intertwine with the characters and plot until we had no choice but to succumb to the manipulations intended by the screenwriter. We had our favorite performers, and tended to look at their body of work as a whole, rather than align the actor with a specific role.

In all honesty, we preferred to never typecast anyone, not even in our minds, because we loathed the idea that someone might see either of us as nothing more than just one facet of our personalities.

When judged by a single trait or characteristic, every human being in the world would be found lacking. It is only when you study the person as a whole can you truly gain perspective about that which they truly are.

Having chosen to adorn the walls of our small, five-doored hallway with images of screen legends, we found ourselves faced with even more unmade decisions. Who would we choose? Which roles would we depict? And, more importantly, where on the wall would each image go?

We spent hours, side by side, combing through the Internet for just the right photograph. First, the image must be black and white, and second, though we were less firm on this point, the image must be of an actress.

Mostly owing to the fact that we would stop halfway our searches in order to watch the movies that had been conjured by the pictures before us, it took about two weeks to finally get the first dozen pictures printed, matted, framed, and hung on the wall.

Early in the process, Prince Charming, in his usual, understated but still over-the-top style, insisted that it was not only the actress that was important, but also the role which she portrayed.

Take for example, Vivien Leigh, Agnes Moorehead, Elizabeth Taylor and Michelle Pfieffer. Most people would reflexively select *Gone with the Wind*, *Bewitched*, *National Velvet* and *The Witches of Eastwick*, respectively. These are well-known works by these very famous women, and almost everyone we welcomed into our home would be able to easily identify the actress.

However, not everyone would remember a purple British Literature textbook from Wormwood Academy, the same text book that the blond bully would knock from my hands nearly every day while I stood outside Miss Smart's classroom waiting for the teacher to arrive and unlock the door. Nor would they remember that toward the middle of this book was a full-page photo of Vivien Leigh as Lady Macbeth, taken for a stage production in Stratford-upon-Avon in 1955. *Macbeth* was the play that turned out to be the key that released me from my first Tower, and, it seemed appropriate that this would be the image that adorned our "Hollywood Hallway."

The fact that I have compared my own mother to the same character on more than one occasion was simply a coincidence, and nothing more.

This detailed analysis went into every single photograph we chose. Ms. Moorehead's portrayal of the acid-tongued mother-in-law on the television series *Bewitched* was nothing short of amazing. The show had been a rerun staple in both mine and Prince Charming's youths, yet we opted for her more earthy performance as a crass, under-educated, long-suffering housekeeper in *Hush, Hush Sweet Charlotte*. Michelle Pfieffer's photograph came from the film adaptation of Neil Gaiman's *Stardust*, the wicked Lamia returning to her quest for eternal youth. Elizabeth Taylor is the one that took the least amount of time, as we had just recently watched *Cat on a Hot Tin Roof*.

To the day that I die, I will swear that Liz, chasing after Brick and Big Daddy in that simple white dress, makes Marilyn Monroe in *The Seven Year Itch* look like a schoolgirl playing dress-up.

Photos were added in bursts—sometimes one, sometimes ten, sometimes twenty. Movies were paused to point out a scene that might work with the current collection, or form a basis for a new one.

Natural groupings began to occur—actresses portraying witches, actresses from the golden age of Hollywood. There was even a section of one wall devoted to three of the women who have portrayed Batman's anti-hero Catwoman, with Eartha Kitt, Michelle Pfieffer, and Anne Hathaway each bringing a unique aspect to the performance.

Tonight, however, is not about the women on the wall in the hall, but about allowing access to one of the most guarded parts of our lives—our home and our marriage—to the women who have joined us this evening.

One of the unfortunate side effects of eloping is that you do not get the opportunity to have a traditional reception, and while I do not regret our decision in the least, I did want to at least gather some my closest friends in our home (something we rarely do) and celebrate our union.

Upon entry into our house one is immediately deposited into the library. Perhaps the former homeowner used it as a living room, but Prince Charming, seemingly the world's foremost fanatic of Disney animation, desired a room like the library from *Beauty and the Beast*. As we do not currently live in a medieval castle, the best solution was to simply line the room with floor-to-ceiling book cases and stuff them with volumes of all shapes, sizes, genres and bindings.

The more we collect, the more we learn about collecting, and now most of our collection is bound in hardback, almost always a first edition, sometimes with the author's signature on the title page.

Three of my dearest friends are sitting casually with Prince Charming, exchanging what I am sure are embarrassing stories of my youth in exchange for a bit more information on himself.

He and Artemis sit side by side, both tall and leggy, with blonde hair and blue eyes. Paired this way, he resembles the legendary twin brother of my first best friend's namesake—Apollo. It is not a bad parallel, as he brings light, music and poetry into my life, and is credited with the long process of healing my wounded heart.

My most closest of friends are collectively called The Goddesses, and each is named after a specific ancient deity with whom they share some commonality.

Next to Artemis sits Persephone, an archaeologist of some renown in her own right, her name chosen mostly due to the frequency with which she descends into the earth. Persephone was a few years behind me at Wormwood Academy, but the difference in our ages made no difference when, two days before my senior prom, I asked her to join me at the event. Nearly twenty years later, she sits in our home, wearing the very dress that she wore to our prom, her form still petite enough that it fits perfectly.

Rounding out the quartet here is Aphrodite, a recent addition to my own personal pantheon. We met while working on a project: she was one of the vendors, I her client. She was only supposed to be on-site for a single day, but her flight home was canceled due to inclement weather. Three bars and one very bad karaoke experience later, we were fast friends. When Prince Charming and I were first feeling our way through the genesis of our relationship, it was to Aphrodite I had turned, questioning the logic and sanity of my actions. She asked simply if I was in love with this man. When I answered in the affirmative, her response was precise, concise, and almost insulting:

"Then be with him, you idiot. Only you would try to apply logic and reason to matters of the heart."

Tonight, Aphrodite is watching, learning, and occasionally interjecting with her thoughts, but their conversation is just a small blur of sound against the noise throughout the house. I can hear a cackling laugh from another room, a laugh that reverberates off every hard surface and into the library.

Choosing to investigate, as well as continue my duties as host, I step into the small den where we spend most of our days. Comfy chairs and a long sofa surround the room on three sides, the fourth wall holding a flat screen television along with cable box, DVD player, a laptop, and, oddly enough, an old VHS player.

Given that we are over a decade into the new millennium, having such an antique definitely makes us unique amongst our counterparts. But, with Prince Charming comes a lot of stuff, and in all that stuff were a lot of VHS tapes, most of them made by the Disney corporation.

I think back to how thrilled I was when I saw the old machine for the first time, and how that happiness grew when I saw his collection of videotapes. I can remember when there were "video rentals" tacked onto music stores, and how every Saturday night my sister and I were bundled off to Turtle's on Old National Highway to pick out a movie to watch that evening. And while DVDs and other digital media may have greater technical capabilities, sometimes there is nothing more satisfying than putting a tape in the VCR, hearing the comforting click-click-click as the spindles turn the wheels, and watching the screen flicker as the tracking adjusts itself for the clearest picture. It will always take me back to simpler, if not necessarily happier, times.

VCR notwithstanding, I would not call the current occupants of this room—Hera and Hestia—antiques. Well, not if I want to continue to be able to do fun things like breathe. I had once been Hera's secretary for a short time, however, our friendship grew beyond the boundaries of traditional employer/employee relationship once I changed jobs. Hestia and I were secretaries together, although not for Hera. Though there are twenty years between their ages, you could not tell that Hestia is in her late thirties, and Hera is staring sixty dead in the barrel.

They both look younger than I do, and I am quite sure Hestia could give Prince Charming a run for his money.

The queen of the Greek gods, Hera is also known as the goddess of marriage. Her current namesake finds herself equal to the title, having been married five times. Hestia, named after the Olympian mistress of the hearth and the home, is a perfect hostess in whatever home finds herself, even if it is not her own. While she may not make the best event planner (fussing with trivial details such as menu planning and decor are not her forté), she possesses the near-unique ability to ensure that the actual execution of the event goes better than originally planned. She can group people, most of whom she has just met, according to mutual interest, and literally move people around to ensure that the intangible energy of every event remains at just the right level. This led me on several occasions to call what she did "manipulative networking."

To say the least, she is my "go-to" gal when it comes time for any company holiday parties or other professional events, and should I be hosting my own party, I set the date based on her schedule, not mine.

One year we celebrated my birthday four months after my actual birthday.

Hera and Hestia, sisters on Olympus and fast friends here in Atlanta, do not need me here, so I continue my journey even further, this time into my own personal space—my study. This is where I retire to get away, where I can do something as important as research, look up a recipe, or, more often than not, play video games. During the (rare) moments when I cannot be in Prince Charming's arms, I love being in this room, with its crimson walls and beige curtains, framed portraits and unframed paintings thrown on the walls in an organized yet still haphazard manner.

I slip into my chair, purloined years before from an office that I begged to have, but realized, once inside, it was nothing more than a metaphorical prison cell—a Tower with Internet service. I close my eyes and let the sounds of the party, still audible through the closed door, wash over me, and I smile.

Prince Charming's braying laugh leaps above the rest of the tableau of sound, and I smile. No matter where he goes, I can always sense his presence, even if it's hundreds of miles away.

If my life were a Hollywood movie, this is where the scene would fade to black, and the music would swell to escort the moviegoers out of the theater and back to their real lives. The quest had been won, true love had triumphed over apathy, and there would be an implication of "happily ever after" that would have held the subtlety of an anvil falling on Wile E. Coyote's head.

More often than not, one does not see the harsh reality that comes along with time. The moments when life's little woes suddenly explode in size and strength to a point where it can no longer be contained, or when illness, be it physical or mental, slowly slithers into the story, moving from supporting to leading role unnoticed until it is too late.

For over thirty years, I have been a pragmatist, bound by the laws of logic, and that side of myself will never completely disappear. While I know that there will, eventually, come a day that will be darker than those that precede it, after that darkness will again come the light.

Light and dark, yin and yang, beauty and the beast. Nature strives for balance, and in Prince Charming, she has found the one that balances me, flaws and all.

If you had asked me right then and right there, as I sat in my chair in my study of our home during a small gathering of our closest friends, I would have sworn that my life was, without a doubt, a fairy tale.

I think of the Towers of my youth, when I was locked away from my classmates, and I realize now that my study could very well be a Tower of its own, but one of my own creation. Its windows and doors are unlocked and thrown open to the world, my rescuer in the next room. I think of the couch in the media room, and how my husband and I spent our first weekend together there, watching movie after movie, the time punctuated by a more than occasional kiss, touch, and caress. We stayed up as late as possible, avoiding sleep so we could be together longer.

In all honesty, while I was surprised when he said he never wanted to leave, I was even more shocked when I realized I never wanted him to go.

I begin to think about the future, and while I know that there is no predestination, I am rapidly becoming a firm believer in Fate. It was nothing short of divine intervention that brought Prince Charming (my "Gift of God") and I (his "Laughter") together, and now that we were one, I never want it to end.

At the core of our union, there is but one insurmountable truth: we have each other. That simple fact makes the tribulations that we would strive to avoid, but know we cannot, all that much easier to bear.

We are but two Ugly Ducklings who managed to find each other. But instead of becoming swans, we celebrate our feathers just the way they are.

THE
LITTLE MERMAID

I AM FORTY YEARS OLD, and I am alone.

The sun has just set behind the hills in front of me as I absentmindedly speed in a nearly-straight line away from Atlanta, the white paint on my recently-purchased Ford Mustang still glowing in the twilight. I have an MP3 player jacked into the car's stereo, a mixture of classic rock and more contemporary pop music playing loudly, though still muted by the sound of the rushing air which is cleaved into the car by the small gap in the window. Although the temperature outside is surely below freezing, the cool air keeps me alert, a necessity on the long, straight roads that are slipping further and further into shadow.

The lanes of the interstate are nearly devoid of other cars, and I am sharing the highway with convoys of tractor-trailer trucks, spread out both singly and in small groups, like Morse code along the road. I remember during my younger days, before Prince Charming, before the Dwarves, before Artemis and Hestia and Hera, when I would drive ridiculously long distances, usually at night. Initially, the semis' size made them imposing and dangerous, but over time I learned not to fear these mechanized elephants on the open road; these are people who drive professionally. It is, in fact, the non-professional drivers whom one should fear.

I set the cruise control, knowing that I am barely one-third of the way through my journey. What is my destination?

I'm headed halfway to Nowhere.

"See ya," said Prince Charming, cocking his head to one side. He turned and walked into the Richard B. Russell Federal Building, the imposing Orwellian edifice that dominated the south side of downtown Atlanta. I had been in the building precisely three times before today: once to enlist in the Navy, once to enter the Navy, and once, to bear witness as my husband had his world torn apart.

The causality of the situation that brought us here today is not my story to tell; that burden belongs to someone else. It is not out of a lack of a desire that I cannot say what happened, but rather a lack of knowledge.

When our world was invaded by those charged with protection, our marriage license was not worth the paper upon which it had been printed. I had to be isolated from my beloved for my own safety, and I had to put my trust in him to make the right decision.

It was simultaneously the easiest and the hardest decision I have ever made. Of course I trusted him, although the indoctrination of my youth would rear its head and scream at my consciousness to change its course.

As I so often do these days, I ignored it.

The government, the all-knowing, all-seeing authority in the land, had reached its decision, and Prince Charming was handed the consequences of his actions on a letter-sized sheet of paper. We returned home, phone calls were made, and then phones were switched off, so that we could spend time with each other.

I really wish the prosecutor would have worn something other than stretch pants on the day they destroyed my Prince's world.

In the days leading up to the kiss goodbye, more than one person had inquired if I intended to continue our marriage. I will admit, I did entertain the thought of divorce for a while right after the whole thing started.

In the end, I can honestly say I thought about it for an entire minute before I made my decision.

Prince Charming did not do anything to me. There was no malice in these actions toward me, and while the story of what he did is not mine to tell, the story of what happened after he went away belongs to me.

By either coincidence or simply feeble-mindedness, I had managed to walk out of the house on the morning he left without my cigarettes and lighter. I managed to bring a book for the train ride home, a bottle of water should I get thirsty, not one but two cellular phones, and my messenger bag.

After he turned and went inside, I stood and watched until he had fully entered the building. I made my way down the handicapped-access ramp, banked on both sides with two huge hedges of pink and crimson flowers, with only a single thought on my mind:

How the fuck did they get azaleas to bloom in July?

I remembered when I worked in downtown that every third door would open into a some kind of convenience store, and I should be able to purchase a pack of cigarettes there. I was so focused on my goal that I, at first, did not notice the increase in my heartbeat, or the shallowing of my breathing.

Apparently, one of the bi-annual "Clean Up Downtown" campaigns must have worked, because I couldn't find a single bodega. After three blocks of walking, I finally reached Peachtree Street and turned left, knowing for sure that though convenience stores may no longer exist in downtown, the Mall at Peachtree Center did.

Miraculously I happened upon a small, cloistered store where they sold tobacco products, and purchased cigarettes and a lighter. While I preferred a traditional blend, Prince Charming preferred menthol; both the green and the red box were handed to me before I even realized that I had asked for both, my request so standard it had become rote.

I tossed both packs and the lighter in my bag, and ran out of the store, the walls already closing in. Spotting the Five Points Station a few blocks away, I kept running until I reached one of the concrete benches that line the outside of the station and collapsed onto it, my breath coming in gasps. I tried to slow my breathing, but could not. Instinctively, I reached into my bag and pull out my cigarettes, shredding the plastic outer-wrap in a frenzy to free the contents faster. I thumbed a single one out of the pack as I dug my lighter out of the bag, but when I attempted to light the cigarette, my hands were shaking so badly I could not connect the flame with the tip of the cigarette.

That's when I saw the shoes.

They were amazing shoes, black, with a rounded toe and tall, stiletto heel. The leg that grew out of the shoes was also shapely, the hem of a black skirt landing just above the knee. I continued to raise my head until I was staring in the steel-gray eyes of a woman who had somehow noticed my plight.

"May I help you with that?" she asked. Her tone was not condescending, but honestly helpful. I held out the lighter to her, and rather than lean forward, she sat calmly on the bench next to me and flicked the lighter on, cupping her hand to protect the flame from the nonexistent breeze. I touched the tip of the cigarette to the fire, and inhaled deeply, the smoke jarring my lungs.

"I have some water if you need some," she offered, again, not in a haughty manner. I turned to her and said that I was simply suffering from "allergies" and that I would be okay.

She had the kindness to pretend to believe me.

As I looked at this woman, I slowly realized how out of place she seemed. One rarely sees professionals on this side of downtown simply wandering the streets with neither files nor briefcase, especially in the middle of the morning, halfway between the start of the day and lunch. Her pale skin was offset by her dark, chestnut hair, which seem to roll off her head and down her back. She turned to me, catching my eyes. After a moment's reflection, I realized that she brought the total number of people that I had seen with gray eyes to two.

"Do you mind if I sit for a minute? These heels are killing me." I nodded my assent. "Thank you."

I looked at her again, not speaking. I am usually quite convivial with strangers, another skill drummed into my head over the years. I looked back at the ground.

We sat in silence for several minutes; the woman simply looked around at the passersby, and occasionally at me. I felt as if I knew her, but was sure we had never met.

"Are you sure you don't want some water?" she again asked, standing, and obviously making ready to leave.

"No, thank you. I actually have some myself." I checked in my bag to make sure.

"Good," she said. "It's always good to be prepared, but even then there are things for which there is no preparation."

"What do you do then?" I asked.

She had started to walk away, but stopped when she heard my voice. "You make a choice. That's really the only wise thing to do."

"What if you choose wrong?" I asked.

She looked at me, and smiled the smallest smile.

"Do you think you chose wrong?"

No, I thought.

"Neither do I," she said simply, then turned and walked away from me, disappearing into the crowd of pedestrians on the sidewalk.

Calmly, I stood, crushed out my cigarette, and made my way into the subway station. I was almost at the turnstile when I caught a glimpse of an owl soaring through the air over Peachtree Street, banking to the southwest, the morning sun on its back.

Over the next few days, I alternately lost my mind, and had my greatest breakthroughs. Three hundred projects were started, and none were finished. Our home turned from "slightly cluttered" to "disaster area" in a matter of nights.

Friends took turns sleeping on the pull-out sofa, but all the support in the world could not alter the most basic of facts: Prince Charming was gone, and the distance between us was causing me physical pain.

In an attempt to straighten up the house (which only resulted in making it more cluttered) I discovered a cigar box on a high shelf in our bedroom. Curious, I pulled it down, and opened the lid.

Inside were silly things, worthless to anyone but him, and now me—an index card on which I had written notes to help keep track of characters while watching a television serial, the Metro passes from our wedding weekend in D.C., a simple scrap of paper with nothing but my name written on it.

Unbidden, the memories tumbled forth, yet instead of the orderly storage system I had enjoyed all my life, the onslaught was chaotic and jumbled. Tears streamed down my face, my ability to control them long lost alongside my appetite and need for sleep. In that moment I knew two things for sure: first, when you separate a soul, it hurts, and second, the next person that asked if I was okay would most likely require medical attention themselves.

How would he have handled this? How would he have made it feel better?

I turned and looked around the room, my eyes coming to rest on the VHS tape of The Little Mermaid. Tears began anew, but they were the more gentle tears that come with happiness. I picked up the cassette, and soon the sound of the sailors' voices singing the opening number filled the house.

I could almost see him standing in front of me, smiling at me.

He seemed proud of me.

If Disney had actually adapted the original tale of the "The Little Mermaid" more closely, incorporating the not only original characterizations and plot, but its not-so-subtle homicidal and suicidal overtones as well, they would have gone out of business due to the parental outrage and subsequent lost revenue. However, the general storyline remained somewhat intact: mermaid rescues prince, mermaid swaps tail for legs, *et cetera*.

One critical concept that the animators left out is how, in the original fairy tale, mermaids do not possess immortal souls; that is the privilege of humans. It is only with true love's kiss that a human soul can flow into a mermaid, carried on their very breath.

Andersen's original story tells of a mermaid who rescues and falls in love with a prince. However, since she is a mermaid and he is a human, cohabitation is a bit problematic. Desperate to share the world of her beloved, she turns to the sea witch, trades her voice for legs, and returns to the human world.

The prince recognizes her, noting that she resembles the girl who had saved his life. Unable to speak, she dances, despite the fact that her movements cause her to feel the pain of a dozen knives stabbing her feet every time she takes a step. The prince soon falls in love with her dancing, but at the behest of his father the king, he is to wed another. The Prince refuses the king's demand, agreeing only to meet, but not marry, the princess to whom he had been betrothed.

Despite the prince's best intentions, this tale has no happy ending.

When the prince meets the princess, not only is she stunningly beautiful, she looks exactly like the girl from his memories, the girl who once saved his life. They are wed immediately, and on the voyage home, the little mermaid vows to end her own existence now that her prince has chosen another.

Her sisters, however, bargain with the sea witch and are given a dagger. If the little mermaid stabs the prince in the heart and lets his blood drip on her legs, they will turn back into a tail. She can then return to her family, her home.

In hindsight, I can understand why Alan Menken did not want to set that version to music.

While my Prince had not married another, there was still a great separation between us. I received lots of letters from him, and sent one each day in return. I tried to be helpful to him whenever I could, and my heart leapt every time he called.

Like Andersen's little mermaid, when Prince Charming kissed me for the very first time, I could feel the breath moving back and forth between our lungs, our souls touching, splitting, and exchanging, a piece of the other settling into his new home in the body of its mate. When he kissed me and roused me from my slumber, I shook off the beige and bland existence of my past and embraced the crimson hue of my future. And when he kissed me goodbye between those banks of flowers in front of the Federal Building in Atlanta, Georgia, he was neither reclaiming the piece of his soul he had given, freely, to me, nor was he returning the one I had given him.

But, just like the little mermaid, my family wanted to have me for themselves.

"I'm just glad we're getting the old version of you back," said my mother casually, and, if my interpretation was correct, happily. "Things will be better."

I stared at her in shock. For a while, I thought she had forgotten that it was my fortieth birthday, until she slipped me a card that stated in bright colors on the front "Better hope mental illness isn't hereditary," and when opened said, "because if it is you're screwed."

It was just as amusing as when she had asked, the previous night, if I watched Orange is the New Black, then kept saying "I'm sorry" over and over again, through peals of delighted laughter.

We were standing in the kitchen of the her house, each of us sipping a glass of water. Well, she was sipping. I was currently considering whether or not to throw mine at her head. I had come over to her house the previous evening to help my father with some odd jobs that required more than one set of hands.

"What do you mean?" Surely, I had misheard.

"You know, the 'you' from before he came along," she said, as if this were explanation enough.

The look on my face obviously told her otherwise.

"Back before Prince Charming, before all this," she said as she waved a hand in the air, as if the spastic gesture contained the whole detail of what she was trying to convey.

Suddenly, the meaning of her gesture snapped into crystal clear focus: she meant me. I knew I had changed as a result of my relationship, but this was the first time since it began that someone had told me that it was a bad thing.

"You know," she continued. I quickly put my cup on the counter as a precaution. "Back when everyone loved each other and everyone was happy."

"There is a flaw in your logic," I said, hoping I could remember how to speak her language.

"What's that?"

"Not everyone was happy," was my response. "I wasn't happy. I was overweight and I was miserable. I kept trying and failing at goals that I had no chance of achieving in the first place, and then felt terrible when I didn't succeed. I... I... I lived in fear of living."

"I just don't understand you," said my mother, exasperation creeping into her voice. "I never will."

"Mother, if you don't get to know me, how will you ever understand me?"

"I just want the old you back," she said. "We really do love you."

I remained silent.

"You know, right?" she asked, her words taking on a harsher tone. "It might not seem like it sometimes, but..."

"Mother, stop."

"Excuse me?"

"Just stop. I'm going home," I said, and went about gathering my things.

"How are you going to get there?" she asked loudly. A legitimate question, because while I had recently purchased a car, used but in great shape, I was still wary of driving alone, especially through the city. Having not driven for years, I had become quite adept at navigating Atlanta's limited but somewhat functional transit system, and it was that system of buses and trains which had brought me out here yesterday.

It seemed that same system would be taking me back to my house as well, and sooner than I expected. The nearest subway station was only a few miles away, a modest distance for someone who is used to being a pedestrian in Atlanta.

"You can either take me to Decatur Station, or I can walk. But there is no way that this day ends well, and I'm getting out while I can."

"What are you, scared?"

The irony of the fact that we were two seemingly rational adults about to play a game of emotional chicken was not lost on me.

"Of course I'm scared," I said, and she started to smile. "Just not of you."

The corners of her eyes crinkled, a look with which I was quite familiar. Things were about to get very loud and very ugly, very quickly.

"Answer me one question, Mother: do you want me to get a divorce?"

She seemed stunned by my request. I repeated it for clarity.

"This one is a freebie, Mommie Dearest." I slowly enunciated every word, "Do you think I should get a divorce?"

"Well, that's not for me to say," she started.

"Last chance. I promise. There will be no reaction on my part whether you say yes or no."

"Whatever you want to do is fine with me," she began, getting ready to launch into another speech about how she wanted me to conform to some preconceived—literally, before I was conceived—idea of the ideal son.

"Thank you," I said, startling her train of thought.

"I beg your pardon?"

"I said 'thank you'," I replied, slinging my bag over one shoulder. At this point, I could only assume I would have to walk. It was a beautiful day outside, and in the distance, I could hear the bells of the First Baptist Church of Decatur ring twice, indicating it was still early afternoon.

"But I didn't give you an answer." My mother seemed confused about this point.

"Yes, you did. You just didn't say 'yes' or 'no'. I still got the answer I thought I would get."

"And what was that?" she asked.

"It's easy to tell everyone in the world what they should do, get upset when they don't do as you say, and then gloat when things fall apart for them. That, however, is not love.

"Love is giving advice, but leaving the person to choose for themselves without repercussions. Love is helping the person back up after they've fallen, even though you pointed out the stumbling block.

"For the record, whether or not you wanted me to get a divorce would not have had any bearing on the matter whatsoever. I was just curious if you would have actually answered the question."

"You and your word games," she sighed. "This is why you don't get along with anyone."

"Mother, I asked you a direct question, free from emotional repercussion, and you still hedged your bets. You know one of the things I love the most about Prince Charming?"

"What could that possibly be?" she sneered, her defenses activating. Oddly, I was not on the offensive; for the first time, I felt the solid ground beneath my argument, and the electrifying charge of confidence surging through me.

For probably the first time in my life, I feel fully confident not only in my argument, but myself.

"He would stand and scream at the storm," I said, proudly, "even if he was dead wrong. He would chase everything in life with a passion that I have never encountered, be it a movie or a book or a toy or... me. Do you know how many Darth Vader toys and gadgets and whatnot I have in my office?"

"I don't see how that could be relevant," she mumbled.

"It's relevant because he pursued me with that same passion, and even after we got married, continued to pursue me with the same level of intensity, if not more. I couldn't stop him from buying those toys, because he knew that Vader is one of my favorite characters, and he wanted me to have all that I could carry. He would bring me a single red rose if he knew I was having a bad day. Did you know he was the first person I have ever been with who actually brought me flowers. I have a drawer full of cards that he gave me, some of them for no reason at all other than to tell me how he felt. He may not be Shakespeare, but I know that he stood and went through every single card in the rack to make sure it said the exact thing he wanted it to say, because he thinks I am worth it."

"I've always thought you were worth it," she said. She launched into her well-rehearsed tirade about sacrifice and disappointment, and while it may very well be all my fault, I had had enough.

I reached into my bag, pulled out the card she had just given me that morning. I held it up so she could see the cover, and she fell silent.

"You gave me a card that jokes about mental illness, when you know damn well Prince Charming is bipolar. I mean, what kind of a person does that?"

"We'll talk about this later," she said, turning to go inside. "I love you!" she calls over her shoulder.

As I turned and started making my way toward the subway station, I knew my mother wanted nothing more than to have her ideal image of her family together, to appear to be happy, even if no happiness exists. There seemed to be no room for Prince Charming in that family portrait, and like the little mermaid in the Andersen tale, I had been told that in order to return to my proverbial sea—

my family—I had to plunge a dagger into the heart of my marriage and watch it die, forever living with its blood on me.

In reality, it was much worse; my Prince had not forsaken me as the little mermaid's prince had betrayed her. It was during those horrible days that we saw our love not only solidify, but grow stronger and stronger, as if it was, on its own, preparing us for what lay ahead. Though they would never say it directly (to do so would be considered rude), I knew without a doubt that my family felt that Prince Charming should be cut out of my life, permanently.

Given the option, I would rather plunge a dagger into my own heart first.

In the end, the little mermaid chose not to kill her love, as I chose not to kill mine. And like the little mermaid, I continue to carry a piece of Prince Charming's soul with me wherever I go, until the day that we are reunited.

This is a marathon, though, not a sprint.

I pulled out my phone and called my friend Jack. He had just recently moved back to town, and we were re-establishing our friendship.

"Meet me at Woof's?" I asked. He lived across the street from the bar, so it's not like it was a long commute.

He agreed, and I told him my estimated travel time. He said he might even go down there and get, as he put it, "warmed up."

I really hoped he didn't; every time he got drunk I wound up wanting to punch him.

Jack was already at the bar when I walked into Woof's on Piedmont, one of my favorite places to partake of adult beverages. He waved me over from the far side of the bar, and as I rounded the corner and sat down next to him, I was reminded why I love this place so much.

Essentially, Woof's was a sports bar that happened to cater to a gay clientele. The patrons of this place came here to socialize, watch a game, and spend time with their friends. Unlike its counterparts down the street at Ansley Square, which reeked of cologne and desperation, Woof's was just a regular bar where one could get a drink with friends.

We sat and chatted, the perfunctory conversation regarding current working conditions, co-workers, families and friends taking just over an hour. Jack decided to take the conversation in a new direction.

"I don't want to offend you by saying this," he began. I immediately cut him off.

"If you have to lead by saying that," I said quietly, "then you may wish to rethink what you're about to say."

Apparently, I was either speaking too quietly for Jack to hear, or he simply chose to ignore me.

"I know you and your mom..." he began, again.

"Mother," I correct.

"Fine, mother," he said, rolling his eyes. "I know you guys had this big fight, and I'm sorry that happened. I really am. But with Prince Charming gone, why don't you just wait for him to come back, and in the meantime, work on your relationship with your family?"

I could not believe what I was hearing. I politely asked him to clarify his position.

"What in the name of all-holy fuck are you saying?" My voice is a tad louder than I had intended, and I've drawn the eye of the bartender. I wave him off, grateful he is an old friend. "I mean, do you understand what you are saying?"

"See, I didn't want to upset you," he said, but for the life of me, it didn't sound like an apology.

Over the years, I have held only a handful of hard and fast rules when it comes to verbal discourse with other people. One of them has always been that if you feel you must warn someone that they might become offended by what you are about to say, you probably should remain silent. For some reason, most people feel that this warning, when delivered prior to the offending speech, absolves them of any guilt associated with hurting the other's feelings. To me, it was as ridiculous as its counterpart, the spewing of a string of insults at someone, cutting them to the very core of their emotions, yet adding "Just kidding!" at the end, once again freeing the speaker, at least in their own mind, from any and all guilt.

At least in the first case, the warning comes before the offense.

The tools of the verbal manipulation trade were very familiar to me, though I chose years ago to no longer wield them. After all, I studied at the knee of a master.

"...but that's really the right thing to do. Prince Charming won't be back for a while, and I honestly feel that you should focus on your family. You don't know how much longer you're going to have with them. Just...just... think of it as pressing 'pause' on your marriage."

"I'm leaving," I stated shortly, pulling out my wallet and throwing two twenties on the bar. I didn't give a damn about getting any change. If I stayed there any longer, Prince Charming would not be the only one of us behind bars.

"Sweetie," he said pleadingly. "Sit back down, we can figure this out. I just think you're putting too much effort into this, when there are other things you can be doing."

Time stopped. I turned. I leaned down and got right in Jack's face, not caring that my breath probably reeked from the two packs of cigarettes I had smoked in the past three days.

"The fact that you think that pressing 'pause' on my marriage would be a good idea is probably the very same reason you have not had a relationship that has lasted longer than the three months it takes for you to get bored between the sheets. I called you because my own mother chose today, my fortieth birthday, the first birthday after Prince Charming went away, when I was already close enough to the edge, to tell me that everything I have felt, from the happiness, to the sorrow, to the ecstasy, to the pain, over the last three, almost four years was just a 'phase' I was going through, and would I please toe the family line. When I called you, all I wanted to do was just wanted to unwind, and maybe, just maybe, get a little sympathy."

"But," he interjected, "I said I didn't want to offend you."

"Welcome to my world," I growled. "It's about time someone other than me didn't get what they wanted."

Before I could say anything else, or give in the temptation to deplete his brain of oxygen until he was nothing but a human vegetable, forced to watch the world but not interact with it, I walked away from Jack.

Orange may be the new black, but it is still a hideous color on me.

The sunlight was bright as I burst out of the front door of Woof's. I was only three steps into the parking lot when I heard my name called from behind me.

Jack really needed to learn when to give up.

"I'm sorry," he said, blinking his eyes to adjust to the sunlight. "I'm worried about you."

"I'm not."

"I just don't understand why this is so important to you," he said, and I felt the rage building inside me again. "I mean, what's the worst that can happen? It's not like you can't go out and find someone else."

I had been trained to abhor physical confrontation motivated by anger, believing it to be one of the most unrefined ways to settle a dispute. But as my fist connected with Jack's jaw, I found that sometimes, a man needed to be a touch unrefined, especially if he wanted to get his point across.

Prince Charming taught me that.

"I don't want anyone else!" I spat, my rage sated for the moment. "He is my **husband**, not an MP3 player. You cannot press 'pause' on a person. To do so would be even crueler than what he's going through now."

"But he's not here," stated Jack, massaging his jaw. He was going to have one hell of a bruise, and part of me was proud.

"A fact I'm acutely aware of," I snarled, my anger beginning to return. Jack was about to be in need of serious medical care if he did not drop it.

"You're just going to get hurt," he shouted.

"I'm already hurt!" I screamed at him. Pedestrians on the sidewalk have stopped to watch our exchange, and soon, someone from the staff of Woof's will be out to toss us off the property.

I decided to save them the trouble, and turned away from Jack, heading toward the subway station. I assured myself that walking away from the confrontation was the right thing to do, and I wove through the semi-drunken revelers that filled the sidewalks of the new Lindbergh Plaza. Once home to nothing but BellSouth's headquarters, a dozen restaurants and bars now catered to all manner of urban professionals. I reached the station and descended to the platform, walking far away from the crowd that has congregated toward the center. I took a seat on the last, hard bench before the platform stopped and the tracks merged back into parallel lines.

The train arrived. I walked on board and took a seat in the nearly-empty car, and soon we were underway.

The silver snake that is the train slithered down its track, and I could see the twin holes bored into the side of the hill which would plunge us underground for the first half of my journey. Immediately, claustrophobia consumed me, my heart racing, and while I knew it to be physically impossible, the train car seemed to be getting smaller. There were only two other occupants in the car, both engrossed in their telephones and paying me no attention.

We were encased in blackness as the train entered the tunnel, and my condition worsened, my heart thudded so forcefully I felt that it may literally burst forth from my chest at any moment. I felt the train slowing as we pulled into the Arts Center Station, but the normally pleasant, female voice listing the local attractions was muted and muffled by my pulse thundering in my ears.

As soon as the doors opened, I bolted from the train, my feet loud slaps on the cement stairs that I took three at a time, desperate to reach the open air beyond the turnstiles. I did not bother using my rail pass to cause the gate to open, but instead used my hand to cover a sensor on the turnstile that causes the gates into swinging outward.

Even after I exited the station, my breathing did not slow. I could feel my heart pulling me in one direction, my family in the other. I walked north on West Peachtree Street, crossing 17th, and wandered into the forgotten park that I remembered from mine and Prince Charming's many trips into town. We would always pass it when walking back to the station, and would sometimes stop and wonder at how it came to be here.

Surrounded on almost every side by either concrete buildings, old brick row houses, or soaring skyscrapers, this forgotten corner of the city had never been developed, but had remained a forgotten corner covered with green grass, surrounded by a hedge, and containing only a single, solitary bench.

I sat on the bench, and fished Prince Charming's wedding ring out of my pocket, turning it over and over in my hands. Tears were flowing freely now, but despite my physical distress, my mind was oddly ordered. I kept turning the ring over and over in my hands, many questions on my mind.

I stood and looked toward the south, where I grew up and attended Wormwood Academy. If I returned there, if I retreated into the past, I knew I would never emerge. For thirty-five years I had tried, and failed, to fit a mold crafted before anyone, including me, really knew who I was. Every time I failed, I thought the flaw lay within me; but Prince Charming had shown me that the problem was, in fact, within the mold itself.

I turned and looked to the east, where most of my family lived, knowing that, despite genetic or marital attachment, and love, whether in small or large measure, my place may no longer be with them. Is it not the child's obligation to venture forth into the world, rather than cower behind the apron of his mother?

I turned and looked to the north, where the shiny people of Atlanta resided, my mother's oft-iterated dream and hope for me. Doctors, lawyers, and urban professionals bound to the lifestyle of the bourgeois elite. Chains and manacles, even if made by Tiffany & Co., are restraints nonetheless.

Overhead, an owl soared from right to left, pulling my eyes to the west. One flap of her majestic wings and the bird was propelled into the dying rays of the setting sun.

I was overcome with a sense of peace and contentment, the very same feeling that washed over me whenever my thoughts turned to Prince Charming, whether he was by my side or miles away.

I thought back to Jack's question, and began to smile, and my eyes mercifully ceased their downpour and began to dry. My smile grew as I thought again of his suggestion to temporarily forsake my beloved, and focus on the relationships in my life in a priority based on expected lifespan.

Suddenly, I was back in Washington, D.C., Prince Charming's hand in my own, as I slipped the ring onto his finger, promising to love, comfort, honor, and keep him, while forsaking all others.

"All others" is actually a very specific term; it means every single person on the planet who is not Prince Charming.

My decision had been made.

I looked upward, casting my thoughts and my cares into the wind that blew through this forgotten little park, and made my first promise of the next phase of my life.

"I'll see you soon, my love."

I slipped the ring onto a chain that I pulled from my pocket, and fastened it around my neck. Tucking the ring underneath my shirt, I began to walk out of the small park toward the subway station, when a flicker of light in the corner of my eye pulled my attention across the street. A squat, three-story apartment building sat there, dropping into ruin, the paint peeling from the trim and the columns that flank the door. Even though there was a sign posted in front of the building that advertised the name of a local realtor, I swore I could see the faint specter of an old man, his wrinkled face staring directly at me from one of the windows on the third-story. I rubbed my eyes, already swollen from the days and days of tears, and looked back to where the old man was watching me. All I saw is a vacant window, paned with cracked glass, and the empty apartment beyond. I turned, and made my way home.

I spent the next several days saying goodbye to friends, packing our possessions carefully in boxes, storing them in a climate-controlled storage unit not far from the house. I did not need these material trappings, and would much rather unpack them with Prince Charming by my side.

Together we could decide what to do with them. I load my new-to-me Ford Mustang, just a few years old with a perfect paint job in pearl white, with only the essentials, and charted the course which would take me to Prince Charming. While reviewing the map, I noticed that he is exactly halfway between Atlanta and the tiny town of Nowhere, Oklahoma. I may have been able to reach him, but I would make sure that I was nearby.

As I pass another tractor-trailer on the westbound lanes of I-20, I realize that it has been more than five hundred days since our bubble was burst, our sanctuary was shattered, and our lives were invaded. It has been over one hundred and fifty days since I last saw those blue eyes, the fear barely contained in an expression that can only be described as pure and total love. Before his entrance into my life, I would have been unable to grasp the concept of fear and love coexisting, but under his patient teaching I have grown to understand more about the heart, and the emotions which it governs.

It has been twenty minutes since we last spoke, the forced happiness in his voice was tinted with a touch of despair. I think of him in pain and the urgency of my new quest increases.

Subconsciously, I allow my foot to press downward on the accelerator, my Mustang smoothly lurching forward. My destination, my goal, and my mission are as clear today as they were on a Sunday afternoon in Kennesaw, Georgia, over a thousand days ago.

Prince Charming had been locked in a Tower.

And it is my experience that when performing rescues, they're best done from the back of a white horse.

THE END

SPECIAL PREVIEW

OF

THE

MISTRESS

OF

PASSION

THE LEGENDS OF THE ANCIENTS

BY

ZACHARY A. CALAIS

PROLOGUE

Philosophers have often pontificated that should a man become suddenly blessed with eternal life, he would go mad from boredom, as the true weight of time pressed heavier and heavier on his soul.

Personally, I find immortality a source of endless amusement.

Make no mistake, I am not invincible. I have not only borne witness to the deaths of many of my kind, but have also orchestrated the demise of several – both those I knew and those I had never encountered. We can feel pain. We can succumb to our injuries.

We can also choose to end our own existence, but on that I most definitely do not wish to dwell. I cannot bear to be overcome with sadness – while tears will not cause my mascara to run, they do make my eyes red, and that color simply does not go with what I am wearing.

Outwardly, I appear almost exactly like the human females of this time, now that the race has finally increased in size and stature, almost to a point which rivals our own. When we first encountered the species, we seemed enormous compared to their diminutive forms. It was our size, combined with our longevity, which caused the humans to refer to us as giants, or angels, or the high elves of fantasy lore.

Or gods.

No one has referred to me as a goddess in hundreds, if not thousands of years. Well, there was that nice gentleman in Cleveland a few weeks ago; although I am quite sure that his adorations were more from the physical perspective than the spiritual.

It is a random weekend night in New Orleans, and despite the lack of religious holiday, long weekend, or other such social cattle call, the crowd on the Rue Bourbon is still massive and sluggish. I could easily transcend this annoyance, leap into the air and leave the press of the humans behind, but this would draw attention to myself, and more importantly, to the differences between my race and the race of men. I have struggled too long and worked too hard to blend in rather than stand out; a feat, I assure you, that was Herculean at a minimum. After all, I am not predisposed to "blending in."

I move gently, subtly, slowly to the edge of the flowing river of people, mindful that I do not come into direct contact with anyone. As far as I am aware, our physical forms are the only characteristics that we share with humans. In every other way we are different – from the way we build our families, to the way we rear our young to the way we honor our dead. From a human perspective, we have "gifts," though to us, they are merely another attribute of our body—the way some people have long hair and others do not have any hair at all.

These gifts of my people are centered around our ability to manipulate energy, not only that which dwells inside each of us, but that which exists around us. Ever since I was a child, I have naturally exuded an energy which draws others of my kind to me – regardless of my actions or desires. I am constantly surrounded by admirers, nay, supplicants, who do not possess the strength to resist my charms.

The concept is not that remote, even to humans. There are always one or two people in any social grouping who can draw others to their cause with simply a smile and a conversation, who can wield eye contact like a weapon. While very rarely the most intellectual amongst humans, their overall balance and well-being drips off them like rain from a sudden thunderstorm, infecting everyone around them.

The more I think about it, the more I conclude these individuals are, in all likelihood some of my long-distant descendants, for during my multi-millennial existence on this world, my lovers have been many and varied, and drawn from a willing pool of both races. I remember when I first encountered mankind, and my energy washed over them, the effect was more severe than it was on my own kind.

The humans would draw closer and closer to me, desiring at first just the smallest touch, which in the old days was given freely. But one touch was never enough, and they would grow increasingly dissatisfied, until they withdrew into isolation, madness, or both.

The bastards never stood a chance.

I am expelled from the street and onto the sidewalk like a fish leaping from the stream to the shore, though, I assure you, with much less water and absolutely no flopping.

Despite my desire to be inconspicuous, I absolutely refuse to do anything with a lack of grace. Fading into the background has always been, and will always be, an utterly alien concept to me. One look at my body will provide evidence of that truth—from my round, full bosom, perfectly proportioned hips, and narrow waist that gently squeezes my form into the shape of an hourglass.

If I live another ten thousand years, I will never understand the humans' propensity for minimalism when it comes to their bodies. They strive to make themselves free from fat, from hair, from blemishes. This seems to be a more recent development – as late as the 1900's to be sure. I remember when a subtle obesity reflected wealth, when body hair spoke of virility, and when scars told of a life that was lived rather than an existence which was endured. Humanity, for all its technical marvels and wonders, has yet to discover the object of its quest – its Golden Fleece, as it were.

Almost every single one of them is searching for a mate.

You might say that I'm an authority on the subject of coupling. Most people, if they truly understood who I am, would say I am *the* authority on the subject, but then, most people would be wrong. I have walked this earth for thousands of years, and I have been known by many names, but my true name lost in time – even I cannot recall what it is. I do not remember much of anything before I was found unconscious on a beach in Cythera, a tiny little island which was my home for several centuries. The people there called me Αφροσίτη, and while the Romans would later call me Venus, most of the world today refers to my ancient self as Aphrodite.

The peculiar little rectangle of plastic in my purse calls me Ayala Montague, although that name was chosen by My Shadow, as she that handles all the arrangements with money and identity that are a requirement for life in the world today. I remember when she had either acquired or created the documents for this identity, and the half-smirk on her pale lips as she indicated the last name of Montague. When asked, she only responded that it was "appropriate," a literary reference from a few hundred years ago. I have a vague memory of a play where one of the lead characters had the same name, but if memory serves, that character was male. Quite frankly, I have never understood her sense of humor.

The night air around me, heavy with humidity, is a tapestry of sound that combines the voices of a thousand men and women, some talking, some laughing, even a few screaming. Strands of music randomly color the pattern, coming and going so quickly that one barely has time to register its existence before it disappears completely. I chuckle to myself at the allusion, for that is how I feel about mortals. Compared to our longevity, the span of a human life is exactly like the music on the Rue Bourbon – you barely have time to enjoy it before it is gone. Mortals have always been my playthings, for I knew I could never build anything to last with them – they simply did not live long enough. Would that my son had held himself to the same standard.

I suddenly stop on the sidewalk. My son. I have not thought about him in years. Make no mistake, despite my romantic dalliances and self-absorbed behavior, I am not without maternal affection. My child, my Little Love. I have not seen him in hundreds of years – since before the conflict that drove me from my beloved Cythera, first to Asia Minor, then eventually to Rome.

The telling of the tale which forced me from my home belongs to another of my kind, one whom I am quite happy never to cross paths with again, although I feel that another meeting is near. Despite my premonition, I hope I never again have to endure the disdain that is permanently etched in those gray eyes whenever their intensity is focused on me. There is only one thing that has the power to make me feel worse than her: the look in my son's eyes when he gazes at me While I know that my son has forgiven me for my terrible wrongdoing, I will never forget the disappointment in his eyes the last time we looked, honestly and openly, at each other.

I remain as a statue on the sidewalk, the river of humanity flowing around me, their minds focused on their own pleasures, making them immune to my distress. I feel a hand clasp around my waist, and I am propelled forward. So lost in my own memories am I that I had not realized someone had gotten so close. *Fabulous*, I thought. *Another suitor for the evening*. Well, there are worse ways to spend the night, and it has been a while since I was last with a mortal. That insurance salesman in Cleveland, I believe. White hair, piercing blue eyes, fumbling apologies all over the place. I do hope tonight's entertainment is more capable.

I snap out of my reverie, preparing my standard set of adorations and invitations, when I suddenly realize that the arm that is wrapped casually around my waist is attached to the body of a man who is everything but a man. He is actually taller than I am, and while recently there has been a mortal or two who has achieved this stature, this is no mortal. The energy that I am releasing is touching a similar force emanating from him, and finding it compatible.

This is no fledgling – there has not been one of our kind born for over a millennium. He is easily as old as I am, although his skin is like that of a newborn – so pale that it is nearly translucent. His eyes, his coal black eyes, bore into mine with the intensity of a man on a life-long quest. Was I the object of that search?

He shifts me off the sidewalk and into one of the narrow, dimly-lit bars that are plentiful in the French Quarter. While at first glance it seemed to be overly crowded with mortals, a couple at a low table in the front corner suddenly remembers that they need to be somewhere else. Whether this was true, or my new companion simply planted the suggestion in their minds is of no importance to me. Our abilities are as varied as our appearances and our histories, and I am grateful for the rest the chairs provided. After all, I have been thinking quite a lot in the past few moments, and I am rapidly becoming exhausted.

One of my own, and an entire evening to play with him. What is a girl to do?

"Who are you?" I ask, my breath finally starting to slow, although I honestly cannot remember when it had quickened.

"Do we really want to do names?" is his response, his eyes coy, and his lips smirking. For all his pallid features, he could have been My Shadow's brother, although I know this was not the case. Despite their being brought into this world simultaneously, they were as different as night and day – literally. "You never do names, do you?"

"Not never, but never often," I reply. "They complicate things."

"So I hear," he answers, his eyes never leaving mine. A waiter approaches, but is waived off by my companion, my Pale One. Regardless of whether or not I actually learn their names, I have to call them something in my mind. "Although, I am only beginning to understand these games that men play."

Through the plate glass by the table, I can still see the crowds pushing and rolling down the sidewalk, although my perspective had changed significantly. I choose instead to do a more thorough examination of the Pale One.

His features, while extremely angular, are not unpleasant. His frame is slight, but healthy. His clothing is nondescript: a black cotton dress shirt paired with black pants, black belt, and black shoes. Normally, this would be a great outfit, especially on someone who is so fair, but my eyesight reveals the signs of wear at the cuffs of his sleeves and the waist of his pants. He has scuffs on his shoes, as if he has been traveling by foot a great distance. I can only assume that he traveled by foot – the power of true flight, while possessed by some of our race, was limited to a select few.

Once again, and just as suddenly as when I was on the sidewalk outside, my thoughts are wrenched away from my control, and again I find myself thinking about my son.

Now he can fly.

Not only can he fly, but there was a time when he flew everywhere. I would tease him that he must believe that if his feet were on the ground for too long, he would never be able to take flight again. Then I remember the day when he could no longer lift himself into the air. Despair began to overtake me.

"Eriyos," I whisper, to no one.

"Excuse me?"

Just as suddenly as I had departed I am back – at a corner table in a bar in the French Quarter on a random Saturday evening with a member of my own race whom I had never encountered. I mumble an apology to the floor.

"Is everything alright?" His eyes are full of concern.

"Of course," I reply, full of strength this time. "I cannot seem to stop thinking of someone."

"Me?"

I laugh. I genuinely laugh.

"Of course not, my dear. We have only just met." Despite his lack of pigment, the Pale One obviously does not lack in confidence. "How did you find me?"

It is his turn to laugh.

"What makes you think that I was looking for you?" As the laughter dispels the tension, I begin to notice more and more about him. His speech is clipped with an accent that I have never encountered, although the longer we live in an area the more colloquial traits we acquire.

"Because you found me," is my response, and I begin to transmit my desire in earnest. Immediately, his eyelids slip to half-mast, and I know he is feeling the effects. Soon, I will feel the return rush, and then we will need to find someplace more... private. But, we have all night.

"If you are not thinking of me," he breathes, his voice quiet, but still loud enough for my enhanced ears, "then is it another lover? Who is Eriyos?"

The name stops my desire cold. "My son."

"Will he be joining us this evening?" the Pale One asks, his eagerness evident in his voice. Apparently, he, like several others that I know, enjoyed the pleasures of both the male and the female. In all my years, I never concerned myself with the desires of others, although My Shadow feels that these individuals are greedy.

"I would say no," I respond, "but tonight seems a little out of sorts. You never know what might happen."

"I do know what I would like to have happen."

"Darling, everyone wants that to happen. Most of the time they are not disappointed."

"Most of the time?" His eyes are curious now. "Why not all the time?"

"Because," I say, becoming apprehensive at his directness. "Because mortals are bound with morals; they restrict themselves to behavior which they believe will bring enlightenment, when all it brings is starvation to the soul. Our kind are fewer and farther between with each passing decade. Because try as you might, you cannot force compatibility. There are a thousand reasons for it to succeed, and an equal number for it to fail."

"I always thought love was eternal. That once you discovered love it was yours, forever." He is becoming lost in his own memories, but I cannot be bothered. I am laughing in earnest now, cackling even.

"Really?" my voice is raised, and some of the nearby patrons have taken an interest in our conversation. I gently turn their attention the other direction; grateful that after all these years of drawing people to me, I have finally, recently, learned to push them away. "Why are you asking me about..."

"Are you not the goddess of…" he begins, but I never want to hear that phrase again. Not after what it cost me. Not after what I did.

"No, my dear, I am not that goddess. I have been many things over the years – the consort of kings of old, the superficial beauty on the arm of the most powerful and the most humble. And when it comes to physical attraction, the manipulation of ecstasy, the enhancement of pleasure, I am most definitely that mistress. But I have never been, nor will I ever be, the goddess of…" I can almost taste vinegar in my mouth as I spit the last word "… love."

He is stunned. His posture seems to draw inward on itself, as if I am his mother and had just scolded him for his stupidity. I see my designs on the evening beginning to evaporate, and after the emotional roller coaster of the last several minutes, I would like very much to give myself over to passion, to lie in the arms of a man of my own kind, who will not collapse with exhaustion after only the briefest of interludes. I want to feel the sun burn down on our skin as we continue well into tomorrow, and perhaps the evening beyond.

"If you want to discuss that subject, my darling," I say, this time tenderly, "perhaps you really should locate my son."

"Why?" was the quiet, almost choked response. Damn. This one might get away.

"Because, he found it. He found it, he nurtured it, and true to form, it did conquer everything."

"How do you know? If you are not, as you say, the goddess of…" I hold up my hand to stop him; I do not want to hear that word again.

"Because, I tried to destroy it," I say simply. "And it conquered me."

COMING SOON BY ZACHARY CALAIS

SOMETHING REDNECK THIS WAY COMES

MY GIRLFRIENDS HAVE ALWAYS BEEN GODDESSES

THE MISTRESS OF PASSION

ABOUT THE AUTHOR

Zachary A. Calais was born sometime in the mid-1970's in Atlanta, Georgia. A lifelong lover of literature, Zachary desired to be an author from a very young age after witnessing his mother drop what she was doing and immediately type a story of several pages. Upon asking why she did so, she simply stated "I had a story that I just needed to write." It was then that he knew he would, eventually, be an author.

As he grew older, he also desired to pay the rent and keep the utilities working, and so he reluctantly entered the workforce, specializing in information technology and graphic design. While stuck in airports and hotel rooms traveling for business, Zachary began penning short stories as a cure for boredom. The stories remained locked in a computer until one day someone pointed out that yes, Zachary did have some measure of talent, and yes, he should really get a move on with "this whole writing thing."

After marrying his own Prince Charming, Zachary maintains a base of operations in Atlanta, but reserves the right to pick up and go at any time and without any notice.